Alvaston Parkes: Chess Detective

"That's it!" He turned back to me. Sophy had just returned and was warming her hands on a coffee mug. "Something happened *in the game*. Something happened in the last five moves that they, whoever they are, didn't want us to see!"

"But they took the game record. We don't know what those moves were," said Sophy.

"Then we'll work them out. Sophy – have you heard of retrograde analysis?"

"Yes, of course, but it's very unusual for it to be applicable in real life."

"Yes it is, but there are features in this game that make me think it just might be possible."

"But what if it was five moves ago, Alvaston?" Sophy was speaking from the laptop screen. "How could anyone possibly work out the last five moves?"

"One by one," he replied.

Alvaston Parkes: Chess Detective

Alexander G. Wilson

Table of Contents

Foreword by Robert Graham

I write this almost twenty years after the events in question: only now, after such a long time has elapsed, has it become safe to divulge even these activities from the very early career of my lifelong friend Alvaston Parkes.

The events in question happened when we were sixteen, during the Spring term of the lower sixth. I mention this to emphasise just how far Alvaston had advanced, both in sleuthing and in chess, at that very early age.

Of course you, as a reader, will want to engage with the puzzles, to pit your wits against a young Alvaston Parkes, but be warned: these puzzles are not for the beginner. Indeed, I have it in mind to write a second volume for the beginner, but this is not it. At the time I embarked on this adventure I had been playing chess for a good few years but, as you will read in these pages, I frequently struggled to keep up with my young friend who had been playing for less than two.

Whatever your playing standard, I would encourage you to have a go, and to facilitate this I have arranged the material quite carefully. Each chapter ends with a chess diagram showing the position with which we were faced, while most of the analysis and discussion are saved for the start of the next chapter to allow the reader to consider the problem without accidentally coming across unwanted hints and clues. I have preceded one or two of the more difficult puzzles with some of the early parts of our discussion to help people get started who are not yet masters in chess detection!

Keeping a chessboard handy is obviously helpful, but I have tried to give enough diagrams to make it possible to at least follow the main arguments without one, and of course if you want you can read this without trying to solve any of the puzzles: the endeavours I describe have shaped the whole of the computer industry as we know it today, although even now I am not at liberty to divulge the full extent of the rippling effects of the events of Spring 2020.

Robert Graham, September 2039

Chapter 1. The Illegal Move

I want to start by telling you how I first met Alvaston Parkes. We actually played on the same team (chess, of course!) but only for a single game. I had just changed schools for the lower sixth and it was my first outing for the school team. Alvaston was a regular – he's by far the best chess player I've ever known, but this was to be his last match for the school, and in a small way it was something to do with me. This is how it happened…

It was a quickplay tournament with fifteen minutes on the clock for each player. Six secondary schools were taking part, with five players on each team. Our school was hosting and we had pushed together three rows of tables in the canteen, each with five boards alternating white and black on each side. We took our places for the first round, which was against Longbridge High School. The players on each side were ranked in order of strength: I was on the lowest board and Alvaston, naturally, was on board one.

I felt nervous; I always did at the start of a match. Everyone else seemed nervous too, all apart from Alvaston, who had a permanent air of indifference, as if his mind was somewhere else. Mr. Wills, our maths teacher, was the umpire. He asked the players playing black to start the clocks. And battle commenced.

I was absorbed in my own game, just glancing occasionally at the board next to me. In the distance I was vaguely aware of Alvaston playing very fast: I thought it unlikely that his game would last the full half hour.

My match – unfortunately – was the first to finish. He chased my king all the way to the opposite end of the board and after only twenty minutes delivered the coup de grace with a loud announcement of "Checkmate!" and we shook hands. A minute later board three won for our side and after a further minute boards two and four finished, with a win and a loss on either side. Two all - it was all down to board one. Everyone, including Mr. Wills, crowded round the board. Alvaston was clearly winning, but he wasn't sitting at the game. He was standing next to my board at the other end of the line, and his clock was counting down towards zero.

With fifteen seconds left Alvaston sauntered back to the table. He joined the crowd and watched his clock reach zero. His opponent sat back in satisfaction and held out his hand. All of the Longbridge High players started smiling and slapping each other on the back – the mirror image of our team, who were shaking their heads in disbelief.

One of our players, Mike Drayer, was fuming. Mike was board two and team captain. He stormed up to Alvaston and got right up into his grill. "What are you doing? We need you to win!"

"I did win," said Alvaston quietly. He was completely unperturbed by Mike's anger, even though Mike was two inches taller and had a much bigger build than Alvaston's wiry frame.

"You were winn…ing," said Mike, separating the "ing" from the "winn". "But your opponent won because you went awol in the middle of the match! You always do this! You might be a good player, but I don't think I can ever remember you actually winning a game for us!"

Mr. Wills brought an end to the conversation. "Quiet! There are still games going on – talk in the corridor if you must!" The other three members of our team left to discuss what to do next. I was new to the team and had little to add to the conversation, so stayed behind in the hall with Alvaston.

When the other games had finished and people were milling around in the break I saw Alvaston sitting quietly at his own game. "What did you mean," I said, "about winning the game?" I wondered whether perhaps he wasn't used to playing with clocks and didn't understand about losing on time.

Alvaston looked up. "Oh, that! I had him on the ropes from move twelve. He strung it out a bit, tried valiantly to fend off my attack, but then he finally threw in the towel by playing Be7 to defend his knight on f6."

"But you lost on time."

"No I didn't. I had four minutes and thirty-six seconds on the clock when he played Be7. More than enough to finish the game."

"But you still lost on time."

"Do you like chess?"

That didn't seem to follow on. I thought I'd lost track of the conversation. "What's that got to do with it?"

"Why it's got everything to do with it – Do … you … like … chess?" He was speaking slowly now, as if I was an idiot.

"Of course I do!" Otherwise I wouldn't be here! I added in my head.

"Good – so do I!" he said, smiling. "Those idiots out there," he said, pointing a thumb towards the corridor, "They don't really like chess at all! All they care about is whether Mr. Wills writes a 1 or a 0 on the scoresheet. A single binary digit – anyway, I find that all rather tedious compared with the weird and wonderful delights thrown up by the game itself."

"What do you mean?" I asked.

"I just played the best game of the season. Have a look at the board."

The position was like this…

Black (Longbridge High, Board 1)

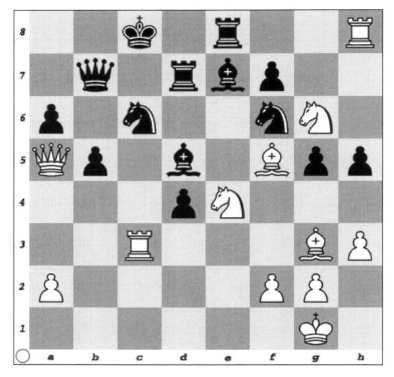

White (Alvaston Parkes)

Figure 1. The final position in Alvaston's game. Alvaston is white and it's his move.

"Well," I said, "he's two pawns up but you've got a strong attack, and you're pinning his rook against his king with your bishop on f5 so you're going to get at least a rook for a bishop. It's like Mike said - you could have won."

"I did win! Look again man, and you'll see that it's mate in one."

I studied the position again. "I can't see it. You can put him in check with the bishop, the rook, the knight or the queen, but he can get out of any of them quite easily: if you take the rook with your bishop he takes back with the king – you get his rook, but it isn't checkmate. Rook takes e8 looks like checkmate, but his knight on f6 can take you back. If you move your knight to d6 (check) he can take it with the bishop and if you move the queen to either c7 or d8 he can take it with his king."

Alvaston looked at me, mildly perplexed. He has looked at me in exactly the same way many times since. At the very least he was surprised I couldn't see it. Or else he was wondering how anyone could possibly have grown up quite so stupid. But he quickly smiled again. "So it isn't any of those moves. I suppose that's a start. Is there any other piece that can deliver check?"

"Ah yes – the knight on g6 can take the bishop on e7 (check). But that isn't checkmate either – black has three pieces defending that square!"

"Does he?"

I looked again, and after a couple of minutes the light dawned. "Oh! I see – black does have three pieces defending that square, but they're all pinned. None of them can take back without leaving the king in check, which is illegal. That's very clever!"

Alvaston seemed genuinely pleased that I was able to appreciate his brilliance. "So you see that Be7 was such an awful move the only possible interpretation was that black had given up the ghost and was tendering his resignation."

"But no-one resigns that way – you knock over your king or offer to shake hands. Isn't it more likely that he just missed it like I did?" *and as everyone else in the room did*, I added in my head.

"Ah yes. Like a dart heading for the triple twenty you have pinpointed and skewered the flaw in my reasoning." He was obviously being sarcastic, but he was smiling so joyously I couldn't hold it against him.

Alvaston thought for a while, as if deciding whether or not to take me into his confidence. "The truth is, once you've reached a mate in one, two, or three, or whatever, the game becomes extremely dull – what's the point of playing out a series of forced moves when you know the ending? And in any case, I got distracted."

"I saw you looking at my game. Is that what distracted you?"

"Yes, as it happens."

"It wasn't that interesting – I screwed up on the king side and he chased my king around. Then, just when I thought I'd got it safe he came up with a move out of nowhere that put me in checkmate."

"Yes, I can see that. In some ways it was quite a clever move. But it was quite illegal. Why didn't you tell him?"

"What? Wait a minute! You only came and looked at my game after we'd finished – you don't know what move he played, and anyway it looked perfectly legal to me!"

"You are correct in that I only saw the position after the game was finished, but you are incorrect when you say that I don't know which move he played. All the information is still there, bound up in the position of the pieces." With that Alvaston got up and started toward my table at the end of the line, where the pieces were still standing in their final positions.

We were interrupted, however, by an announcement that the next round was about to begin. I quickly hurried back to my board and took a photo of the final position before setting up the pieces ready for the next round. How did Alvaston know what my opponent's last move was, and how did he know it was illegal?

The rest of our team came back into the canteen and made straight for Alvaston. "We're all agreed," said Mike. "Playing strength is determined by points on the board, so you're playing board five from now on." Mike was still bristling, keyed up for a fight, but Alvaston was unperturbed. "In that case," he said, "I must respectfully resign my position as a member of the team." And with that he turned on his heels and walked out of the room.

Alexander G Wilson

Black (Longbridge High, Board 5)

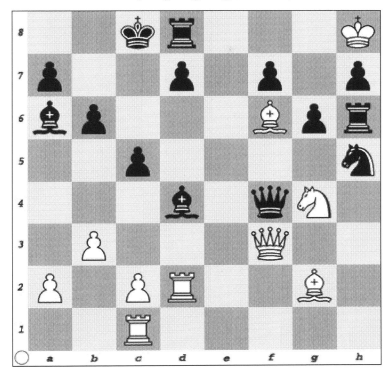

White (Robert Graham)

Figure 2. The final position from my game. I'm white and black has just moved. How did Alvaston know what black's last move was, and how did he know it was illegal?

Chapter 2. Still Illegal

I hardly saw anything of Alvaston in the next five or so weeks. He, of course, was in the top maths set, whereas I – no slouch at maths I might add! – was in the second set. He didn't do chemistry: there were rumours that he had done something in year 10 – something about an experiment that went out of control, though no-one could tell me exactly what had happened, and Dr. Packman had told him he was "never once to set foot in any of my chemistry labs ever again!" We were in the same physics class, so our paths did cross occasionally, but even there he looked permanently bored as if his mind was elsewhere. I only saw him to talk to on a couple of occasions at the chess club.

Then one evening in mid-February, just after tea, we get a phone call. Mum takes it, and after saying hello puts her phone briefly on mute and says "It's Mr. Parkes – you know, Alvaston's dad. He wants to talk to me in private." She shrugs as if to say she doesn't know why either and moves into the dining room, closing the door behind her.

It was obviously something to do with me – I racked my brains to see if I'd said anything to Alvaston that he might have taken offence at, but as I said we'd hardly crossed paths in five weeks. After half an hour mum came back out into the lounge. "That was Mr. Parkes," she said, though we already knew that. "He's asking whether Alvaston can come and stay with us for a while. Robert – what do you think?"

Robert was me, but before I could say anything Dad answered for me, "You mean Alvaston Parkes? I'm not sure about that. He's been in trouble with the school several times now." Dad was on the parent-teacher board and picked up the gossip – perhaps I should have asked him about the chemistry experiment. "He sounds like a bit of a handful - I don't think it's a good idea for him and Robert to hang out too much."

Mum was about to say something else, but the phone, which she was still holding, rang again. "Oh, hello Nigel," she said, and hurried back into the dining room after mouthing 'Mr. Wills' silently in my direction. Stranger and stranger!

After another half hour mum came out again. "We don't really have much choice," she said, "His mother has passed away (did you know that, Robert? – I didn't) and his father can't look after him for the next few months."

"Months!" Dad and I exclaimed together. Alvaston was an interesting character, but months! I am an only child and used to ruling the roost. I wasn't at all sure I wanted anyone staying with us that long.

"It's something to do with some disease or other." I should explain that this was just before the first of the glodemics. We didn't call them that then: 'global pandemic' was the official phrase. "Apparently the government has got wind of a strange new virus out in the Far East, which they think might spread all over the world. According to Mr. Parkes we might all be stuck at home for weeks on end. Mr. Parkes is what they're calling a 'key worker' and has to be on call 24/7, so he can't stay home to look after his son."

"That's a likely story," said dad. "A new virus that's going to spread everywhere… and Mr. Parkes is self-employed in something or other. How does that qualify him as a 'key worker'?"

"I thought the same thing," said mum, "and I told Mr. Parkes we'd discuss it, but Mr. Parkes said he'd ask Mr. Wills to talk with us."

"And what did Nigel say?" That was Dad again – as usual no-one was interested in my opinion.

"That's the strange thing – he said that he knew Mr. Parkes really well, and confirmed the story about him being a widower and said that if he says a virus is coming we can trust him implicitly. He also said that Alvaston is a bit troubled, like you said, but has a good heart and would be really fun for Robert to be with – they could play chess together."

"Why does it have to be us?" Dad again, though I was thinking exactly the same thing.

"Mr. Parkes said that Alvaston had specifically asked to stay with Robert. He didn't know why, but Alvaston refuses to consider going anywhere else." Mum and Dad both looked at me questioningly. Finally it was my turn to speak, but all I could do was look back blankly. I had no idea why he should choose to live at our house.

"I still don't like it," said Dad, "What did you say?"

"What could I say?" said Mum, "I said yes, of course we'd be happy to help out."

Dad sighed, but got out his diary. "OK – so when's he coming?"

"In about half an hour," said Mum. "We'd better get the spare room ready." Mum likes causing a stir, and I think she enjoyed the look of pure horror on both of our faces.

***

Alvaston arrived by Uber exactly half an hour later, with a small carrier bag stuffed with tee-shirts and underwear, two laptop computers and five heavy duty suitcases stuffed with books that Idiot here got volunteered to lug up to his new bedroom, although it looked more like a library after he'd taken out the wardrobe and replaced it with an ad hoc bookcase made of bricks and planks that Dad found in the garage. He wanted to replace the chest of drawers with a desk, and offered to buy one on-line, but mum said he needed somewhere to put his clothes, so instead he worked out a system where he could partially open the top drawer of the chest and tap on one of his laptops perched on top while sitting semi-comfortably on the bed.

It wasn't until late into the night that we finally got the room the way he wanted it, and my parents left us alone in the room.

"So why did you want to come here?" I asked bluntly. It was the question I'd been longing to ask.

"We met at the chess tournament – remember? I thought we got on rather well, old chap!"

"But you hardly know me - we only spoke for twenty minutes or so!"

"Exactly!" said Parkes, pleased. "We spoke for about twenty minutes and we got on rather well."

"So what?"

Alvaston sighed, "Truth is, not many people last that long and still get on well with me." I assumed he was joking, but when I thought about it I couldn't remember him chatting or chilling or just hanging out with anyone at school. I wasn't sure what to say.

Alvaston brightened up, "Anyway, here we are – just open that suitcase, will you?"

I opened the last remaining suitcase, and to my surprise it didn't contain books, but a whole jumble of objects, some electronic, some not, many I didn't recognise, and … a chess set. I fished it out and put it on the bed. Parkes opened the box holding the pieces and scattered them across the board. "Now, here is the final position from your last game." I was amazed that he could remember the position – it was my game and I couldn't have set it up without looking at my phone. "You were asking, remember, how I knew what the last move was and how I knew it was illegal."

"Well it was my game," I said, "so I know black castled – rather sneaky, I think. I thought I could take his rook with my bishop on f6, but I couldn't because his bishop on d4 has my bishop pinned against the king – so that was it, checkmate! But I can't see how *you* knew that was his last move."

Black (Longbridge High, Board 5)

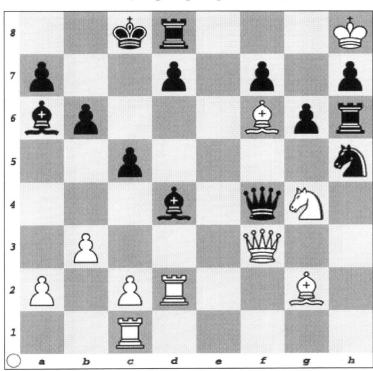

White (Robert Graham)

Figure 3. The final position from my game in the chess tournament. Black has just castled to give checkmate.

"As I said, all the information is still there in the position, like a murder mystery. You just have to work out what happened. Have a look at the position and tell me what you can deduce."

"Well," I started, playing along, "I'm in checkmate. My king is trapped and I can't move."

"That's true, but not relevant," said Alvaston. "Tell me which piece put you in check."

"The rook - black castled, as I said."

"So the rook put you in check. The key question is then 'if that wasn't the last move, where else could the rook have moved from to put you in check?'"

Slowly the light dawned. "Ah, I see! It couldn't have come from the left or from further down the d column because there are pieces in the way. And it couldn't have come from further along the back row because I would have been in check already, which is impossible!"

"And there is nothing that black could have moved out of the way to give discovered check," added Parkes.

I thought for a minute. "Couldn't it have taken something?"

"That is really good thinking, old chap. Very often in retrograde analysis, or retro-analysis as we call it now, the key lies in the pieces that are no longer on the board."

"Retro-what?"

"Retrograde analysis – the study of what *has* happened, as opposed to what is *going to* happen. I've got a book about it somewhere."

"Oh - so it could have taken something?"

"No – not in this case – quite impossible! Even if it took something it still had to move from somewhere and the same difficulties apply. Nice try, though! You're really getting the hang of this. Oh, and by the way, we call them 'files' not columns, and 'ranks' not rows – I don't know why, it's lost in the mists of time."

I let that go – I had a more important question. "And why was the move illegal?"

"That's easy. Your bishop is covering d8. The laws of chess state that you can't castle out of check. You can't castle into check, and you can't castle *through* check, and that applies whether or not the piece is pinned. QED."

I was somewhat chagrined – I knew that rule, but it hadn't occurred to me in the heat of the game.

Alvaston kept on looking quizzically at the position. "Tell me, were there any promotions during the game?" I must have looked blank because he added, speaking more slowly this time, "Did either of you get a pawn to the end of the board and promote it into another piece?"

"No," I replied, "that's pretty rare, isn't it?"

"Yes it is, but it's not impossible, so I couldn't rule it out. In that case, even without the bishop, black has played an illegal move."

With that, he whipped my black-squared bishop off the board and replaced it with a pawn of the same colour. He looked in my direction. "Black's last move still has to have been O-O-O (checkmate) but it's still illegal - why?"

I stared at the board, but nothing came to me. "I give up! The bishop isn't there anymore so black isn't castling through check, or from check, or into check. It's a perfectly legal move!"

"Are those the only laws of chess with regard to castling?" Alvaston aimed a teacher's questioning look in my direction. He seemed amused by my confusion, but it wasn't amusing to me.

I restrained myself and said matter-of-factly "You can't castle if you have previously moved either the king or the rook, and you can't castle if there are other pieces in the way. But there weren't any other pieces in the way – I was there, remember? And there's no way you can tell whether either the king or the rook has moved."

"On the contrary, dear chap, I know for a fact that the black king has moved – unless, of course, you are in the habit of letting your opponent make illegal moves."

I stared fruitlessly at the board. "I can't see it! I can see a hundred perfectly legal last moves for black. Only two involve the king – and I know he didn't play either of those."

"And there may have been hundreds more before white's last move. No – I can't tell you whether it was last move, or the move before, or any particular move. All I can tell you is that at some time earlier in the game black moved his king, and then moved it back to e8."

I was about to boil over with exasperation and tell my new 'friend' exactly why no-one could last more than twenty minutes with him when my dad knocked on the door. "It's two o'clock in the morning!" he whispered urgently, "and you've got school tomorrow."

"Sorry Mr. Graham," said Alvaston, "We lost track of the time." I don't know if Alvaston knew about my dad's misgivings, but he was unfailingly careful and polite with both my mum and my dad.

I left and went to my own room, still thinking about my latest chess conundrum.

Alexander G Wilson

Black (Longbridge High, Board 5)

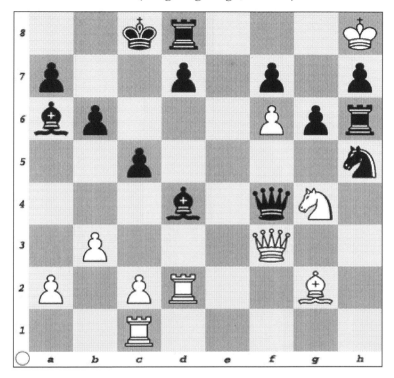

White (Robert Graham)

Figure 4. Position with a pawn replacing the bishop on f6. Black's last move still has to have been O-O-O (checkmate) but it's still illegal - why?

Chapter 3. The Limacine Move

The next day was a Thursday when Mr. Wills opened up the maths room during the lunch hour for chess club. Alvaston was already there with the position set up from the previous night. "Have you solved it yet?" he asked happily.

"Not yet," I replied, not eager for a repeat of last night's conversation.

"This might help - look at the position before black castled." And he 'uncastled', leaving the position below. "There have been no promotions, remember. How do we know that black's king must have moved?"

Black (Longbridge High, Board 5)

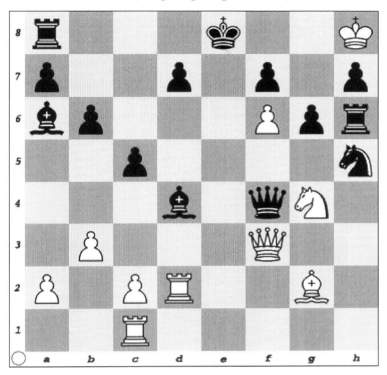

White (Robert Graham)

Figure 5. Position just before black castled. "There have been no promotions, remember. How do we know that black's king must have moved?"

I must have looked completely helpless because he quickly added "Alright – in the real game, how did black get his rook to h6?"

"Well it came from h2 – before the knight moved to h5 of course."

"And how did it get to h2?"

"Well, it – oh! I understand now! Even with the pawn on g6 rather than g7 there's still no way the rook could have got out of the corner. The pawn on g6 could have let the bishop out, and the knight can jump over pawns, of course, but the rook couldn't get out unless the king moved – and I remember now he did move his king to d8 and only moved it back to e8 later in the game."

"Good! Well done!" said Parkes. "I do believe you're getting it."

I was still a bit annoyed by his tone, but intrigued by this new way of looking at the game. "You said someone wrote a book about this retro-something-or-other. Can I have a look at it?"

"Oh no!" Alvaston laughed, "it's far too complex for you!"

He must have seen the colour rising in my cheeks because he quickly added "... for *us*! I meant to say it's far too complex for *us* because you know - we're still beginners at retrograde analysis."

Now he was being patronising as well as insulting. My eyes narrowed.

"Oh dear," he said, "I keep forgetting that sometimes people actually prefer to be lied to than to be faced with an uncomfortable truth." I think he was speaking to himself, but then he turned to me. "I'm sorry, old chap - I thought I'd learnt that after that incident with Mike in year 10."

It turned out that the Mike in question was Mike Drayer. The captain of the chess team Mike Drayer. The big and bulky and easily angered Mike Drayer. And even more importantly the sitting at the table right next to us at chess club Mike Drayer. Everyone in the room jumped as he stood up suddenly from his game, pointed straight at Parkes and snarled "And I'll deck you again if you don't shut up! Some of us are trying to play real chess here!" and with that he sat down again.

Mr. Wills quickly stepped in to prevent a confrontation. "Yes, keep it down, lads, let people concentrate."

***

Tea that night was burgers and chips – my favourite - and we were all eating together at the table. Dad hadn't spoken much to Alvaston and I was surprised when he addressed a question to both of us. "I heard there was something of a fracas at chess club today." How did he know these things? "Something to do with Mike Drayer." Ah yes, Dad was friends with John Drayer, Mike's dad.

"Yes. It was all to do with some sort of altercation Alvaston and Mike had in year 10. Alvaston was going to tell me about it." Alvaston frowned at me. I'm sure he would have kicked me under the table, but that's quite hard when you're sitting right next to each other. I didn't care – I was still fuming from our own conversation at the club.

"I'd heard something about that," said Dad, "What was it about Alvaston?"

Alvaston was caught by the direct question from Dad. He composed himself. "It wasn't my proudest moment. It was after the club knockout tournament in year 10. I'd only just taken up chess, and I was quite pleased to make it through to the final."

"… where you played Mike," I guessed.

"Right. I won, of course, but that wasn't the problem. The problem was what I wrote afterwards in my school blog."

"Which was?" asked Dad.

"The thing was that the last move he played was - literally - the worst move on the board, because it was the only move that led to mate in one."

"So what did you write?" pressed Dad.

"I wrote 'With a mate-in-one available only a man of limacine intellect would have selected instead the only move leading directly to checkmate for his opponent.' The next day he found me at breaktime and left me on the ground with a bloody nose."

We were all confused. "What does limacine mean?" asked Mum.

"Funnily enough the headmaster asked me the very same question. I said it means slug-like. The headmaster said that was a very unkind thing to say, and I explained that Mike wasn't very bright and I was banking on him not knowing what it meant… and he didn't, although it turns out he did know how to use an on-line dictionary."

Dad was still frowning but couldn't entirely suppress a smile.

"Anyway," continued Alvaston, "the really unfair thing was that he was the one who hit me, but I was the one who got suspended!"

Dad cleared the plates and took them into the kitchen, moving as fast as possible, I suspect because he didn't want us to see him laughing.

"Well I hope you learnt something from that experience," said Mum.

"Oh yes," said Alvaston brightly. "I didn't want that to happen again, so I learnt two things. Firstly, I learnt not to say unkind things to people, even if they're true."

"Very good, that's important," said Mum. "And what was the second thing?"

"Over the next Summer I studied pugilism to the exclusion of all else. No maths, no history, no chemistry even, just the simple and pure art of boxing. That's how I got this," he added, pointing to his nose, which was indeed quite out of shape.

"Maybe not quite so good," said Mum.

"On the contrary, Mrs. Graham. The very next year Mike and I found ourselves in the self-same situation, but with our roles reversed. This time he said something nasty to me, and I was the one who left him on the ground."

"So you hadn't learnt your lesson, then?"

"That's exactly what the headmaster said! And what was really unfair that time was that - even though our roles were exactly reversed – it was me who got suspended again!"

Under his breath Alvaston added, just loud enough for me to hear, "though I did leave him out cold with a broken jaw." I was glad that neither of my parents heard that addition!

"So have you learnt your lesson now?" Mum wasn't to be put off.

"Yes, Mrs. Graham. I have realised that violence is the recourse of the dullard and the scoundrel. I have made it a rule never to start a fight, and I have kept out of trouble (well, that sort of trouble anyway) ever since."

Mum seemed satisfied, especially when he added "May we leave the table, Mrs. Graham? I would like to show Robert the final position in that game. I think he'd find it interesting."

"You are very polite," said Mum. "Robert is only ever that polite when he wants something." And she looked pointedly in my direction.

***

When we were upstairs Alvaston quickly set up the board.

"I'm black, Robert, and as you can see it's mate in one – in fact his last move has presented me with a choice of 4 moves, all of which deliver checkmate! Now, you heard me say that Mike was threatening checkmate himself and you can see that Qxf7 (checkmate) would still be possible if I hadn't got there first! And you also heard me say that his last move was the *only* move leading to a mate-in-one for me. Those are the only two facts you need to solve the problem."

"What problem?"

"What exactly was his limacine move?"

White (Mike Drayer)

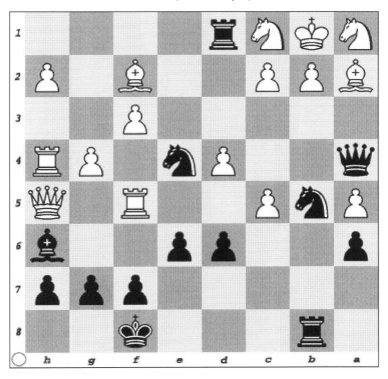

Black (Alvaston Parkes)

Figure 6. "Mike was threatening checkmate himself, and instead played the only move leading to a mate-in-one for me. What was his limacine move?"

I wasn't expecting it to turn into another lesson in retrograde analysis, but the problem intrigued me and I was determined to solve it on my own. Parkes busied himself on his laptop, whistling cheerfully to himself while I studied the board fruitlessly for a good twenty minutes.

"Alvaston," I said, finally, "I can't work out the relevance of him threatening mate-in-one. It suggests that he didn't move his queen or the rook on f5, but he could still have moved either of them from a position where they were already threatening checkmate."

"True! That's an excellent observation, Robert!" Alvaston spoke enthusiastically but continued to stare fixedly at his laptop. "That fact does limit the options for his last move, but not very much. In this case the relevance of his threatening mate-in-one is simply to make it clear that he wasn't himself in check – if you're in check you have to move out of check, which means that you can't have a mate-in-one. Of course there are some rare positions where you can get out of check and deliver checkmate in a single move, but a quick glance at the position shows that isn't possible in this case." He was still staring at his computer.

"But white isn't in check."

"White isn't in check *now*, Robert, but he might have been before he moved. He might have moved his knight to c1 to block a check from my rook on d1, or he might have used his white squared bishop to take a pawn on a2."

"And why is that important?"

"Because, Robert," Alvaston lifted his head to look in my direction, "that would allow trivial solutions to the problem. If white is in check, he might only have one or two legal moves, and it would hardly be a surprise if only one of them led to a mate-in-one for the other side. The 'beauty' of Mike's move," Alvaston motioned with two fingers on either hand to indicate the quotation marks around the word beauty, "is that he had a range of options at his disposal, including a mate-in-one, but instead selected the *only one* that led to checkmate in one for me."

Alexander G Wilson

White (Mike Drayer)

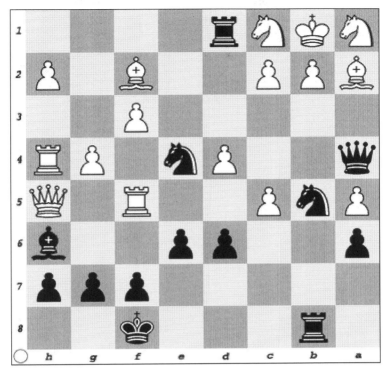

Black (Alvaston Parkes)

Figure 7. "Mike was threatening checkmate himself, and instead played the only move leading to a mate-in-one for me. What was his limacine move?"

Chapter 4. Social Distancing

I remained for over an hour locked in battle with the problem Alvaston had set me, until finally I began to make progress. After a further ten minutes I was confident enough to speak. "I do believe I've got it!"

"Fantastic!" Alvaston almost shouted. For all his seeming cheerfulness while I was floundering around at the start he was genuinely pleased that I had managed to solve the problem. "Tell me your solution - and even more importantly, how you know it is the only possible solution."

"Right," I started, "first of all, as you pointed out earlier, in the final position you are actually threatening checkmate with four different moves."

"Yes," said Parkes.

"So the surprising thing is not that he found a move that allowed checkmate, but that there weren't any number of moves that would allow checkmate."

"Excellent summary of the situation, Robert. It's really important to first of all pin down the features of the problem that require further analysis."

"So it's likely that before white moved none of those moves threatened checkmate at all."

"Yes - but likely isn't good enough. You have to *prove* that I wasn't threatening checkmate."

I thought for a few seconds. "OK, then, take the pawn on c5. That doesn't interfere with any of the mating threats. So if you were threatening checkmate he could have played c6, still leading to mate in one, which would violate the second fact, that the move he did play was the *only* one leading to checkmate."

"Yes, I'll accept that. It's not quite a proof – it could be that his last move was to move the pawn itself to c5, but that would still violate the second statement. Please carry on."

"So, before white moved, none of the four moves was checkmate. I think it's obvious that none of the pawns alter the situation, so his last move cannot have been with a pawn."

"Correct! You're doing well!"

"The queen could have moved from g5, where it stops the bishop from supporting Rxc1 (checkmate) and covers the d2 square to prevent Nd2 (checkmate) but it doesn't stop either N(b5)c3 (checkmate) or Na3 (checkmate)."

"Yes – in fact we only need one possible checkmate - all you need to say is that wherever the queen moved from it could not have covered Na3."

"Yes – that's simpler," I agreed, and decided to rephrase the rest of my explanation. "Neither of the rooks could have moved from a square preventing Nd2 (checkmate), so white didn't move them last. Similarly the black-squared bishop, even if it came from e1, can't have been preventing Na3 (checkmate). So that only leaves the two knights and the white squared bishop. The white squared bishop could have moved from b3, which means that Na3 is no longer checkmate, but it couldn't have been preventing Rxc1 (checkmate) or Nd2 (checkmate). The knight on c1 couldn't have been the piece that moved, because white would have been in check, and we've already deduced that white wasn't in check because he wouldn't have been threatening mate-in-one."

Alvaston interrupted me, "Did you consider that the knight, in moving to c1, might have taken something? Then he wouldn't have been in check."

My face fell – I hadn't even thought of that. I looked back at the position. "No – that's not possible, because the only black piece that's missing is the white squared bishop, which obviously can't have been on c1, because it is a black square!"

"Nice try, Robert, but it could have been a piece promoted from a pawn earlier in the game."

I thought again. "But even a promoted queen would still be delivering check, and we know that can't happen!"

"Yes – good thinking again, but you don't have to promote to a queen. What if black had promoted to a bishop or a knight?"

"Why would he want to do that?"

At that point Parkes descended into a long monologue about the vital importance of proof over conjecture. I won't repeat it here because I'm confident the reader would find it as boring as I did, though Alvaston seemed quite incapable of picking up the yawns and other signs of tedium coming from my direction.

I held up a hand to cut him short. "OK – so it could have been a promoted bishop or knight."

"No of course it couldn't!" Alvaston seemed almost indignant. "I was just asking you whether you'd thought of the possibility."

I was frustrated beyond belief but kept calm. "So it couldn't have been a bishop or a knight."

"No – that's obvious, because all of white's pieces are still on the board."

"But it's black that we're talking about, and black's missing two pawns either of which could have been promoted!"

"But pawns can only change file by taking something, and given that all of white's pieces are still on the board no black pawn can have changed file. The only missing pawns are from the b and c files, and there's no way they can have gotten past the pawns on b2 and c2, which clearly haven't moved – so black can't have promoted a pawn to anything."

So all the talk about people promoting to bishops or knights was a complete waste of time. I would have said something to that effect, but I was desperate to avoid another monologue.

"Anyway," continued Alvaston, oblivious to my frustration, you were about to tell me what his move actually was!"

At last we were back to the interesting bit. "Oh – yes – the only piece left is the Na1, which can only have come from b3. At b3 it protects the c1 and d2 squares, so those moves are no longer checkmate, and it blocks the b file so that the pawn on b2 is no longer pinned when the black knight moves to c3 or a3, so those are no longer checkmate either."

I moved the knight to b3 to illustrate my point.

White (Mike Drayer)

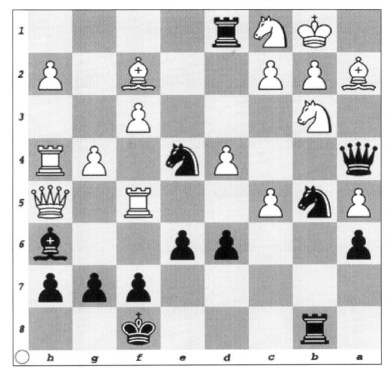

Black (Alvaston Parkes)

Figure 8. "The position was like this. He played Nh8 and the game was up!"

"But even if the knight was on b3, does it satisfy the second condition, that Na1 was the *only* move leading to checkmate in one?"

"Yes. It is easy, I think, to see that no other piece in this position can move to create a mate-in-one for black, so the only alternative we have to consider is Nd2, which is the only other square open to the knight."

"And?"

"And that blocks the bishop from supporting Rxc1, so that isn't checkmate, and none of black's knight moves are checkmate because the king now has a flight square on a1." I sat back in satisfaction, happy that I had completed my quest.

"Perfect, Robert, well done! That was exactly the position. He played Na1 and the game was up!"

***

I hardly saw anything of Alvaston for the next couple of weeks. He would always head straight up to his room after school. "Homework" was all he would say if Mum or Dad asked what he was doing up there. All I knew was that every time I walked past his room and the door was open he'd be sat on his bed staring at one of his two laptops – the one with the black lid. And with every passing day he got more and more frustrated. He stopped going to chess club, and he didn't even want to talk or to play chess in the evenings.

Then, suddenly one night, he brightened up considerably. He even knocked on my bedroom door, which he very rarely did, and as soon as I opened it he announced "I've got it, Robert! I think I've got it!"

Needless to say I had no idea what he was talking about. My first thought was that he'd got the new COVID-19 disease that people were talking about. It was all over the news by that time, this mysterious illness that was starting to spread all over the world.

"What have you got?" I asked.

"The solution!" he exclaimed proudly. "The thing I've been working on for the last two weeks!"

"You told Mum and Dad that you were doing schoolwork!"

"I said I was doing homework, Robert. Schoolwork is trivial, and easily knocked off during break and lunchtime. No, I've been doing homework. Working from home: home-work: it's all in the name old chap!"

"Alright, so what have you been working on?"

"All in good time, my boy, but first I must introduce you to the delights of 'social distance chess'. Come on!" And with that he led me back to his room and got out the chess set. He set the board up in the usual fashion. "The rules of social distance chess are exactly the same as normal chess," he began, "except for one thing. You're not allowed to move a piece to any position that is horizontally or vertically adjacent to another piece of either colour."

As always, Alvaston was talking as if I was as excited as he was and couldn't wait to be initiated into this new form of chess. In actual fact, my interest level at the beginning rated little above 'mildly intrigued'. Then I remembered that the alternative, waiting for me back in my room, was a General Studies essay on 'Conservation and Plant Diversity.' Suddenly my interest in social distance chess skyrocketed.

"But diagonally adjacent is OK," I said to keep the conversation going.

"Diagonally adjacent is OK, yes… and that's it, really!"

We played a few games, just to get the hang of it. The first few came up with some really odd situations that wouldn't normally occur, but after a while the games became pretty similar: the pieces spread out all over the board and the number of legal moves became smaller and smaller as more and more squares became adjacent to occupied squares, leaving not much to do on either side but to repeat moves.

"That was an interesting idea, but in the end it's pretty boring," I said, hoping that Alvaston wouldn't take my feelings about the game too badly.

"Yes," said Alvaston, enigmatically, "That's rather the point." He was as bright as ever and not at all offended.

"So why would anyone play it, and what's it got to do with the success you were crowing about earlier in the evening?"

"All in good time, dear chap. First of all, I want to make sure you've really got the hang of social distance chess, because you'll need it to follow what I'm about to tell you."

With that, he set up the following position. "Black has just played d6, Robert. What is White's best reply?"

Black

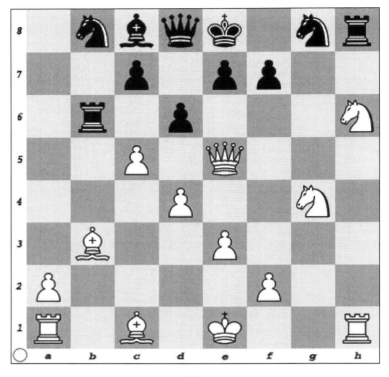

White

Figure 9. Social distancing chess. "Black has just played d6, Robert. What is white's best reply?"

Postscript to Chapter 4 – A Difficult Problem!

Many years later, in a casual conversation while sitting together in the chess club, our discussion turned to reminiscences about those early years and Alvaston confessed that he had lied to me about the position in his game with Mike Drayer.

"White never had a pawn on f3," he said. We were at the chess club, and he set up the actual position from the game. "You can still prove, though, from the same two statements, that the only move he could have played was Na1. I apologise for the deceit, but you were only a beginner in retrograde analysis at the time, so I added the pawn to make it obvious that black hadn't promoted to a bishop or a knight."

I have summarised the conversation here in a postscript because, as Parkes had rightly pointed out, it was far above my ability at the time. It is probably beyond my ability even now, but at the same time I want to show just how far Parkes – even in his school years – had advanced in retrograde analysis.

White (Mike Drayer)

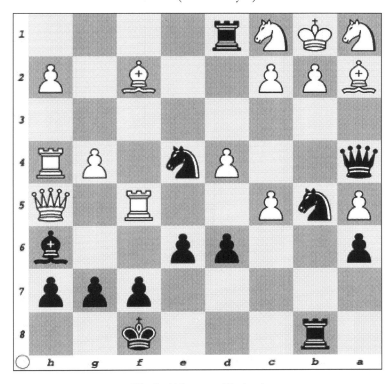

Black (Alvaston Parkes)

Figure 10. The actual position from Alvaston's game with Mike Drayer.

I looked at the position for a bit. "The missing pawn doesn't make any difference to the basic analysis," I surmised.

"That's right – the only question we need to consider is whether black could have promoted earlier in the game to allow the white knight to move from b3 to capture a knight or bishop on c1, and we can knock the knight on the head fairly easily."

"How can we do that?"

"Well, with a knight on c1 the position looks like this," said Parkes.

White (Mike Drayer)

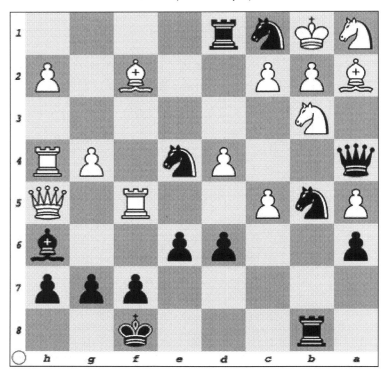

Black (Alvaston Parkes)

Figure 11. Position with a black knight on c1.

"None of the original threats are checkmate," Parkes continued, "but black has two different moves, both of which are checkmate – can you see what they are?"

"Well, Qxa2 is one of them because it's now protected by the knight on c1," I said, pleased to be able to contribute, "but I can't see another one. Black has a new discovered check if he moves the knight away from c1, but white can interpose his own knight on c1, so it still isn't mate in one… oh!

Unless black takes the knight on b3 – then it's discovered check and white has nothing to block it with!"

"That's right. Now you'll remember that white can't be under the threat of mate-in-one before his move because any waiting move would keep that threat alive, and we know there was only one possible move allowing mate-in-one, so we can discount the knight."

"That only leaves the bishop, but with a bishop on c1 there is no immediate threat of checkmate. It can't take the knight on b3 so any discovered check can be blocked by the knight."

White (Mike Drayer)

Black (Alvaston Parkes)

Figure 12. "That only leaves the bishop, but with a bishop on c1 there is no immediate threat of checkmate."

"That's right, Robert, and this is where it gets interesting! With only one capture, which of black's pawns could have promoted?"

"Either the b pawn or the c pawn, as they're the ones that are missing."

"Superficially, yes, but in theory it is possible that one of the pawns currently on a6 or d6 comes from one of those files, and the original a or d pawn was the one to promote."

"I suppose so, although neither pawn could have got past its opposite number."

"Perhaps, although it is likely that white's pawn on c5 came originally from e2, and the e pawn from the c or d file, so at some point in the game black's e pawn might have had a clear run. Fortunately for us, it doesn't matter. The crucial question is not which pawn promoted but on which square did it promote? And with only one capture there are only two possibilities."

"Black must have promoted on d1 or a1."

"Excellent! And d1 is clearly impossible."

I thought about this for a while. "No – I can't see it - why is that, Parkes?"

"Look at the board – black has two black-squared bishops! That means that one of them has to be the promoted piece, but d1 is a white square!"

That was obvious – I felt a little foolish. "What about a1?" I asked, "that's a black square."

"There's the real beauty of the problem," said Parkes. "Yes black could have promoted to a black-squared bishop on a1, but we have already noted that the white pawn on b2 hasn't moved, so there's no way it could have gotten out to be either of the black bishops currently on the board, so that too is impossible!"

Even then, many years later, I was astonished by his chain of thought, but the realisation that he had worked all this out in our teenage years, having only played chess for a couple of years, was positively chilling.

Chapter 5. Champion's Error

Alvaston had posed my first social distance chess problem: "Black has just played d6, Robert. What is White's best reply?"

Black

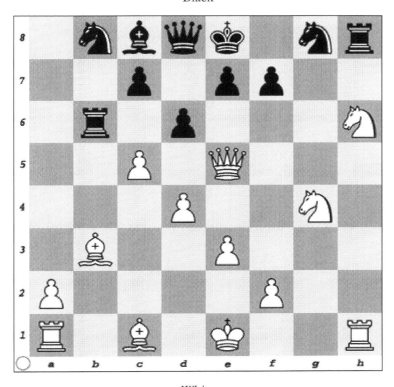

White

Figure 13. Social distance chess. "Black has just played d6, Robert. What is white's best reply?"

"Well," I began confidently, "the most obvious move is Qxh8, winning the rook, but I suppose that's too obvious."

"And totally illegal!" added Alvaston. "White can't take the rook because it would put his queen next to black's night, which is illegal in social distance chess."

That quite knocked the wind out of my sails. "Yes, of course it is. Um, Bxf7 (check) would normally be a good move, but white can't do that either, or Nf6 (check)…." I looked in Alvaston's direction to see if I could detect any change in facial expression to indicate I was on the right lines.

"Go on," said Alvaston, impassively.

"White could take the rook on b6, but then black would take the white queen on e5."

"Something a bit more direct," said Parkes, who for the first time seemed to be getting impatient with my lack of progress.

"Well Ba4 is check, but black can interpose… No he can't! That's it, isn't it? Ba4 is checkmate, because any of the pieces he could interpose would be standing next to another piece, which is illegal, and the black king can't move to f8 because that is also next to the pawn on f7!"

"Well done, Robert. A bit round-the-houses but you got there in the end."

***

With that, Alvaston went suddenly sombre. He went to the window, looked out briefly, and then to the door. He poked his head out of the doorway, looked left and right, and then closed the door quietly.

"What I am about to tell you, Robert, is of national importance."

Of course I thought it was a joke, a schoolboy prank, but Alvaston wasn't one for pranks, and I had never seen him this serious. "What do you mean, 'national importance?' Have you found a girlfriend?"

"I am serious, Robert, on my honour. I cannot tell you what I am about to say unless I have your solemn word that you will not repeat it to anyone. Not the chess team. Not Mr. Wills. Not the headmaster. Not even your parents."

Now it was getting really weird. "OK – you have my word." I was serious. I don't give my word lightly.

Alvaston stared straight at me, as if finally deciding whether or not to take me into his confidence. "I'm not just playing around with this social distance chess. The Home Office asked my father to look into it, but he's rather busy at the moment so passed it on to me."

I have to confess I was very sceptical, but I held my tongue.

"Social distancing is something the government is about to announce to combat this new disease that's breaking out. Everyone will be required to keep two metres apart when they venture outside – if they're allowed outside!"

"What, every time they go out? That's ridiculous!"

"Desperate times call for desperate measures, Robert. This disease is coming, and it will be bad – the government is gradually bringing people up to date with what they know, but most people don't know yet just how hard it's going to be."

I thought about that. It was clear from his facial expression that Alvaston was relaying what he thought was the truth. "What's that got to do with chess?" I asked.

"The government has secretly asked their scientists at Porton Down to make a numerical model of this 'social distancing' measure – is it feasible in parks, or in shops? Will there be an impasse in subways as people try to move in both directions? But real life is very difficult to model, so they needed something simpler to start with – something complex enough to be relevant, but simple enough to be entirely deterministic."

"Chess!" I wasn't really believing the story, but I couldn't help getting caught up in his excitement.

"Exactly! Porton Down invented social distance chess and put out a tender for companies to model the game using a computer and simulate ten million games, calculating certain statistics as they go. It's called Monte Carlo analysis. Only companies carrying this out successfully can bid for the *real* prize."

"Which is?"

"Which is a billion-pound contract to provide computer support for modelling social distancing in real life."

"Wow! But what's this got to do with you?"

"Two big behemoths of the FTSE100 are vying for the project, Tarin electronics and Champion computer services. Put simply, one of them has accused the other of cheating."

"The rules seem pretty simple. How can you cheat?"

"As proof that the companies had actually simulated the games Porton Down stipulated that they be sent the position in each game after a certain number of moves. They then ran each position through their computers to check that no pieces were adjacent to each other unless they were in their starting position."

"That sounds pretty foolproof."

"Well, Tarin Electronics says not. They say that Champion has simply randomly generated these positions and hasn't simulated the games at all. So, for the last two weeks I have been studying each position in detail, applying retrograde analysis to determine whether the games really have been simulated."

"Ten million games! You might be smart, Alvaston, but you can't have analysed ten million positions in two weeks!"

"Of course not! I asked for a sample to be sent over. I limited it to ten thousand."

"Ten thousand!"

"Yes – the point is that retrograde analysis, although extremely powerful, is only useful in a limited number of circumstances. I spent hours and hours looking through positions in which there was no way to tell whether or not they came from a real game."

"And then?" I knew what was coming.

"I found it, Robert! A position that looks at first sight like a feasible position, one that obeys all the rules, and yet could not have been arrived at in a proper game!"

Alvaston started setting up the board to show me the position. While he was doing this I asked, "So what are you going to do?"

"I've already done it, old chap. As soon as I found the position I told my father and he's passed it on to the Home Office. Champion will be removed from the competition. It might sound harsh, based on just one position being wrong, but there could be lives at stake here, Robert, and this type of behaviour can't be allowed when it comes to the real-life model."

He finished setting up the pieces. "There!" he said, sitting back. "White to move. How do I know this hasn't come from a proper game of social distance chess?"

White

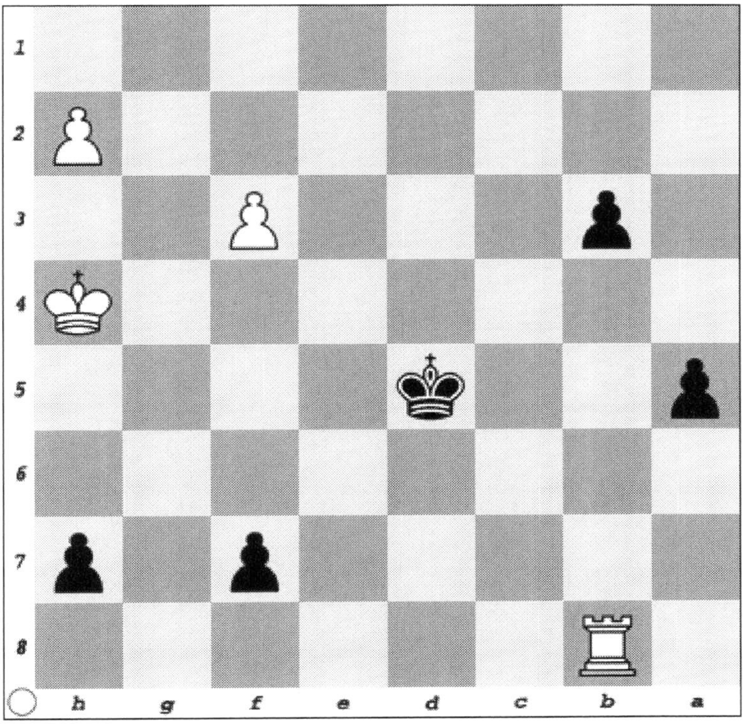

Black

Figure 14. "White to move. How do I know this hasn't come from a proper game of social distance chess?"

Chapter 6. The Coded Message

"I just can't see it, Alvaston!" As usual I was getting exasperated. "There are hardly any pieces on the board. None of them are touching each other and there are myriad possible last moves, none of which contravene the social distance rules."

White

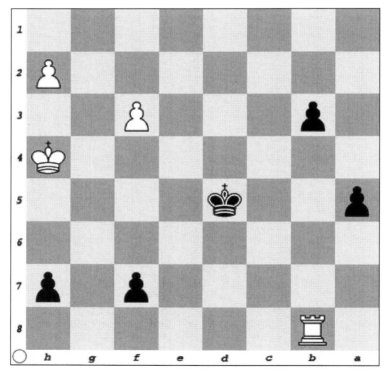

Black

Figure 15. "White to move. How do I know this hasn't come from a proper game of social distance chess?"

"Nonetheless, I can prove beyond doubt that at some point the rules have been contravened – if indeed this position comes from a real game at all!"

"How? I can't even get started!"

"The key is the pawns in the bottom left-hand corner."

"Neither of them has moved, I can see that, but how does that help us?"

"With the pawns where they are, how did the black knight get out?"

"I thought about that," I said. "It couldn't have got out, but that just means that it was taken while on its own square. It couldn't have been taken by a knight, since it would have had to come from a square next to one of the pawns, but it could have been taken by a rook like the one on B8, or even coming down the g file after black's g pawn had moved out of the way."

"Exactly. As usual you are on the right lines, Robert, but not going deep enough! If that's what happened to the knight, how did black's rook get out?"

"It moved horizontally, after the knight was taken, of course."

"So, importantly, the rook was still on its starting square when the knight was taken?"

"Yes, I guess it must have been."

"Then the piece that captured the knight must have moved next to the rook, which is against the rules in social distance chess!" Parkes sat back triumphantly.

"So you see," he added, "she was right all along!"

"She?" Alvaston hadn't mentioned anyone specific before. "Who is 'she'?" I asked.

Alvaston blanched for a brief instant. It was clear that, despite my promise of secrecy, he hadn't intended to share this extra piece of information. But he quickly pulled himself together and continued as if nothing had happened. "'She' is the head of technology acquisition at Tarin Electronics. She was the one who tipped off my father that Champion was cheating. And, as a matter of fact, you know her." He tapped a few keys on his laptop, which sat perched on top of the chest of drawers. Lifting it down he turned it round to show me the photograph of a young lady, no more than our age. She had long black hair and slightly oriental eyes and nose. Quite beautiful, in fact.

"Sophy? Sophy is the head of technology acquisition?" I had only met her once, but I recognised her straight away. She had been at the chess tournament – in fact she played board one for Woodlands School, who went on to win the competition. There was a picture in our school magazine of her lifting the trophy at the end.

"Yes. That's why I wanted so much to play in that tournament, to check out whether she's as clever as they say she is. Her family owns the company, you see, and I wondered whether or not she'd really earned the position."

"And had she?"

"Yes – she's there by merit."

"Wait a minute - you mean you were spying on her?"

"No, of course not, that would be most impolite! I was merely playing chess and keeping my eyes open at the same time."

"So that's why you walked out!" I was putting two and two together. "You were expecting to play her as board one, but when you were demoted to board five, you knew that wouldn't happen."

"Well, yes, and the fact that playing board five wouldn't be much of a, um…" [I play board five, and he must have seen my eyes narrowing] "…um, what I mean to say is playing board five would still be extremely challenging, of course but, um…" At this point he ran out of steam. I bit my lip and determined not to take offence - at least he had tried!

After a brief pause, Alvaston continued, "Anyway, I had already found out what I needed to know."

"How did you manage that?"

"It was all down to you, dear chap, leaving that delightful little conundrum at the end of your game. While everyone was crowded around my game I was standing at the back of the room observing Sophy, who was in turn studying your position intently: after she had finished I went over to see what had caught her interest. I have no doubt that she saw the same thing that I did, that your opponent's last move had to be illegal."

"That hardly proves she has what it takes to head up a key department in a huge multinational."

"No, it's not proof exactly, but there is a particular type of intelligence for which I have observed a very strong correlation with chess playing ability – at least for those who have been introduced to the game at an early age."

"And what sort of intelligence is that?" I asked.

"Why, the one that counts, of course!" Alvaston replied, with a smile and a half-wink.

***

It was just two days later when Alvaston came bounding into my room, full of energy like a greyhound after a rabbit.

"It's her. She's sent me a text." He held out his phone, and I read

'SOME THINGS R F8. WHAT'S THE Q?'

Beneath it was a chess position.

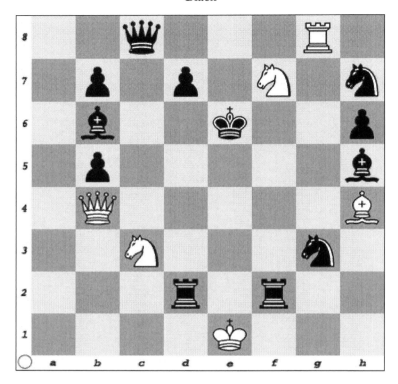

Black

White

Figure 16. "Some things R F8. What's the Q?"

I fetched my chess set from the bookcase and set up the position.

"Some things are fate. What's the question?" Parkes mused to himself while looking intently at the board.

"What does she mean by 'what's the question?'" I asked.

"Well, in interesting chess positions there's always some tangible question. It could be a backward-looking question, like in your game, where we could deduce that the king had moved sometime previously, or it could be a forward-looking question, like a mate-in one or something like that."

"But she hasn't even told you which side is to move!"

"Yes – good point, Robert! That does point toward retrograde analysis, but you can't be sure!"

After half an hour I could see that this problem was well beyond my pay grade – how could you find an answer if you hadn't even been given a question! So while Parkes continued to sit silently staring at the position I turned my attention rather begrudgingly to my homework.

Alvaston sat there, stock still, fingers steepled in front of him, for what seemed like forever. It wasn't until after ten, when both chemistry and physics homeworks were safely in the bag, that he turned to me with a look of triumph on his face. "I've done it, Robert. I know the question! It is forward looking – and it's a mate in two!"

"But you don't know whose move it is – or can you work that out somehow?"

"No, of course not! It's quite impossible in this position to work out whose move it is. But that's the beauty of the problem – it doesn't matter whose move it is. If it's white's move, white has mate in two. If it's black's move black has mate in two. That's why it's 'fate' – it doesn't matter whose move it is, it's still mate in two."

I looked at the position with renewed interest. Now there was a proper question perhaps I could identify for myself the moves leading to the mate in two for each side. My thoughts were interrupted, however, by a question from Alvaston.

"But *what* is fate? What is she trying to say with this puzzle?"

I looked up. "I think she is saying it's fate that you two should go out together."

"Because it's a 'mate-in-two'? That's a bit of a jump, Robert. Lots of chess problems are 'mate-in-two' but it doesn't mean people are asking each other out all the time."

"It's like you said before, all the information is bound up in the positions of the pieces." I couldn't resist a tiny joke, quoting Alvaston's own words back at him.

Parkes looked again at the position. "Well, it's quite an unusual position. Not many pawns, pieces symmetrically placed…"

I thought I was going to lose him for another two hours, so I blurted out the answer, "The pieces have been placed in the shape of a heart, you idiot!"

Parkes turned back to the board and saw that I was correct. "You're right!" he said. "They're in the shape of a heart!" It was only then that the truth of the situation hit him. He said nothing. His face drained of all colour. "She's asking me out," was all he could manage to get out. "She's asking me out, Robert – what does that mean? What do I do?"

I have known Alvaston for very many years now, and in all that time I don't think I have ever seen him so discombobulated. He had lost all of his usual composure and – surest sign of all – he was asking me for help. As you have read in these pages Alvaston had already asked me any number of questions in schoolmaster mode, but this was the first question to which he didn't yet know the answer. I determined to help him as best I could.

"Well, do you like her? Do you want to go out with her?"

Alvaston thought for a moment. "Well she's brilliant." High praise indeed from Alvaston Parkes who, I had noticed, rarely used the word brilliant except in reference to himself. "And very pretty."

"That's a good start, but it's not enough. There has to be something else," I said.

"Like what?" He looked genuinely stumped.

"I don't know – there's got to be something else, deep inside, something you don't feel for anyone else."

Alvaston sat still for a moment. "Yes – I do believe there is!" he said.

"Right!" I said. "You're in love." I was yet to meet the love of my life, but I spoke with confidence, because that's what he needed at that point.

"So what do I do?" he asked again.

"You need to send her a reply to say yes you're interested in getting to know her better."

"Just like that? It sounds a bit stark to me."

I put my head in my hands. "No – not just like that. You need to say it subtly, like she did to you when she sent that puzzle. And not straight away, either – you don't want to sound too keen. Wait a day or so, and then send her a text."

"Perfect!" said Parkes, relieved. "That will give me time to come up with something!"

Black

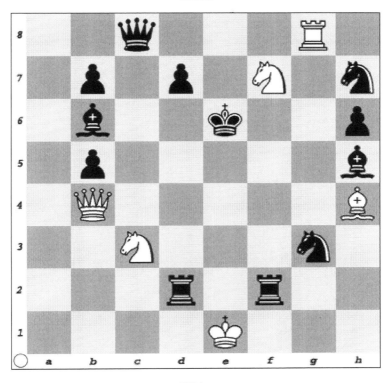

White

Figure 17. Solve the mate-in-two for white if it is white to move, and for black if it is black to move.

Chapter 7. The Coded Reply

The next day I was still struggling with the position Sophy had sent to Parkes. I waited patiently until after tea that evening to quiz Parkes about it.

"Alvaston," I said, having set up the position, "I can see the mate in two for white – Qe7(check) forces the black king to f5, after which Qe5 is check mate."

Black

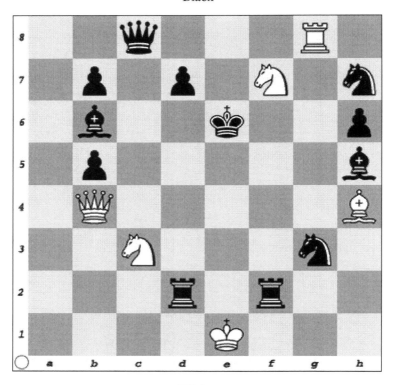

White

Figure 18. Solve the mate-in-two for white if it is white to move, and for black if it is black to move.

"That's very good!" he replied, "It's always harder to spot a move that puts your pieces behind enemy lines."

"But I can't see the checkmate for black," I continued.

"Tell me what you've found so far," said Parkes.

"Well, first of all I think the first move has to be one that puts the white king in check. If black plays a preparatory move like Rh2 that doesn't deliver check, then white has any number of interposing moves that put black in check and prevent him from mating in just two moves."

"Fantastic!" said Parkes. "You are exactly right. The first move must put white in check."

"But there aren't that many moves that do that – in fact the only moves I can see are with the two rooks."

"Right again. You've almost solved it!"

"But Rf1 isn't checkmate because white has Kxd2, and I can't find any move to put him in checkmate on d2."

"Yes."

"Black can move either rook to e2(check), but the knight on c3 just takes it. I thought at first that once the knight had moved black had a killer blow with Qc1, but once the knight has taken on e2 it is covering the c1 square."

"Right again – that only leaves one move."

"Yes – Rd1(check) but the knight on c3 is covering that square too, so can simply take the rook and that's the end of the attack."

"Hmmm." Alvaston moved the black rook to d1, and then captured it with the white knight. "Look again."

Black

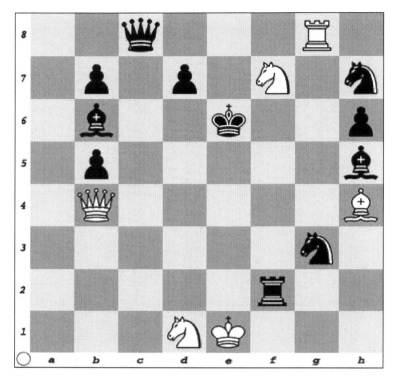

White

Figure 19. Alvaston moved the black rook to d1, and then captured it with the white knight. "Look again."

Now, as a mate-in-one, it was much simpler. "Ah! I see now," I said. "It's Re2, isn't it?"

"Absolutely right! Black's first move forces the white knight off its protective perch on c3, so it's no longer covering the crucial e2 square, and at the same time forces it *onto* the d1 square, which would otherwise provide a safe haven for the white king. Quite clever, I think!"

"Alvaston," I said as I packed away the pieces, "have you thought about how you're going to reply to Sophy?"

"No, not yet — but it's chess club tomorrow. Maybe I can work something out in a similar vein to her communication."

***

The physics experiment just before lunch the next day lasted quite a lot longer than usual, mainly because I was paired with Alvaston and he insisted on doing something quite different to what the teacher had planned. As a result we were late to the club and a number of games were already in progress. We wandered over first to the teacher's desk where Mr. Wills was playing a new recruit. He was quite small, most likely to be a year seven.

Parkes opened the conversation "Good afternoon. I see you're teaching this young chap the same way that you taught me." The young chap looked pleased at this – everyone knew that Alvaston was the best player in the school, and many of the younger players aspired to be like him.

"Yes. Alvaston, Robert, meet Alex Donaldson. This is his first time here, and he's picking the game up really quickly. He could be a future champion!" Alex smiled again.

I was looking at the position. The pawns were scattered across the board, but the major pieces all stood in their starting positions. One of the white pawns stood exactly in the middle between the two squares d6 and e6.

"It looks like rather an odd game," I commented.

Alvaston answered in place of the teacher. "When Mr. Wills teaches chess he starts with just the pawns, and then introduces the other pieces one by one. So this must be Alex's first ever game?"

"It is," said Mr. Wills.

"So played in accordance with the normal chess rules, but with each side moving only pawns?"

"That's right," said Mr. Wills. We're not paying too much attention to the game of course, just seeing how the pawns move really, but yes it's been a perfectly legal game.

"Then that pawn must have been knocked," said Parkes, "please may I adjust it for you?" Mr. Wills nodded, and Alvaston reached across to move the pawn to e6 before adding "Well, we'd better let you get on with your game," Alvaston continued, "I can see it's your move and we've kept Alex waiting long enough."

With that we moved on, and since everyone else was already playing we set up to play a game ourselves – or, rather, I set the board up. Alvaston was busy on his phone.

"So, have you thought of anything yet to say to Sophy?" I asked when he'd finished, keeping my voice low so that no-one could hear.

"Yes – just now. That game between Alex and Mr. Wills. It's perfect!"

"But that wasn't a very interesting game – it seems to have been mainly just shifting pawns around the board. What was so special about that position?"

"I think we're about to find out," he replied. I looked up to see Mr. Wills walking towards us, with Alex in tow.

"Alright, Parkes, I give in. How did you do it?" said Mr. Wills. "You had only just come into the room, definitely after Alex made his last move, so how did you work it out – you've always got some sort of explanation."

We hadn't yet started our game, so Alvaston swept the pieces off the board and quickly set up the position from memory.

Black (Alex)

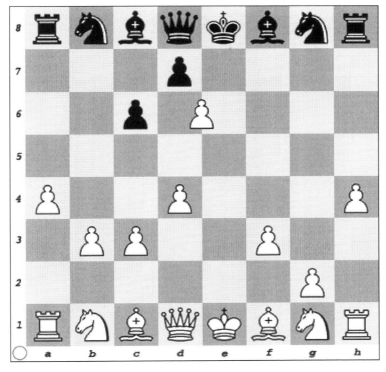

White (Mr. Wills)

**Figure 20. "Alright, Parkes, I give in. How did you know it was my move?"
said Mr. Wills.**

"Now, do you mean 'How did I work out that the pawn belonged on e6?' or 'How did I work out that it was your move?'"

"Both!" said Mr. Wills. "But let's start with how you knew it was my move. I really can't see any way you could know that just from the position."

"I think Alex can help us with this one," said Alvaston. "In a game of chess, Alex, who makes more moves, white or black?"

"White," said Alex, "or both the same if black makes the last move."

"Exactly!" exclaimed Parkes, "That is the heart of the solution."

Mr. Wills went back to his desk to consider this new clue, taking Alex with him.

I was interested in Alvaston's latest tour de force, of course, but I was even more interested in his love life. Once more I kept my voice low "You're going to send that position to Sophy? Why?"

"Mainly because it confirms that I've understood her message. This problem is almost the mirror opposite of the one she sent me: in her position it didn't matter who was to move, it was mate-in-two either way. In my problem you can't tell anything much about the future or the past - the *only* interesting thing about the position is that you can say with complete certainty that it is white to move next."

I was about to speak, but he added enthusiastically "Plus, I've added a caption: 'Who's move is it?' That's like asking how she wants to play things from here."

"You've added – does that mean you've already sent it?"

"Yes – I did it while you were setting up the board for our game."

I wasn't at all convinced that Sophy would be able to interpret Alvaston's complex message from a single chess problem, but if it was sent it was sent and there was no point in trying to make him see sense. In any case, I was saved from having to reply by Mr. Wills walking across for the second time.

"OK, Parkes, I've looked at the position from every angle. I can't see any way that you can tell whose move it is… but I have a sure-fire way of determining the answer before you go to your next lesson."

The bell was just a few minutes away. Parkes looked suitably impressed. "How will you do that, Mr. Wills?"

Mr. Wills smiled. "You're both in detention until you tell me exactly how you worked it out!"

Chapter 8. The Affair on the Siberian Rail Carriage

We all laughed. Mr. Wills was joking, of course, but Alvaston started to explain. "Let's start with the position of the pawn. You taught me the same way, don't forget, and these pawn-only games are really quite interesting. One immediate point is that pawns can only change file by taking something, and in this case, with all the other pieces still on the board, that means taking another pawn."

Black (Alex)

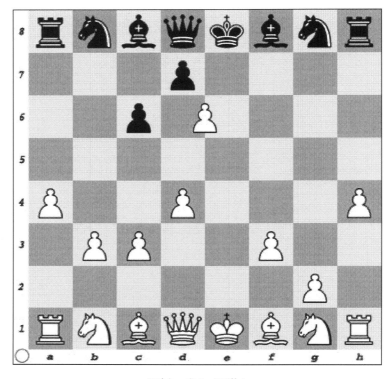

White (Mr. Wills)

Figure 21. How did Alvaston know that the white pawn belongs on e6, and how did he know it was white to move?

Parkes sat back, as if everything were now crystal clear, but when he saw the rest of us looking blankly at each other he leant forward again and continued his explanation, "So a pawn can leave a file, either by taking another pawn or by being taken itself, but the only way a new pawn can move onto a file is by taking one of the pawns that was already on the file, which leads immediately to the rather surprising result that in such a game as this there can never be more than two pawns on the same file! Hence the pawn has to sit on e6."

"Clever!" said Mr. Wills. He moved the pawn to e6. "Now, what about the fact that it was my move?"

Black (Alex)

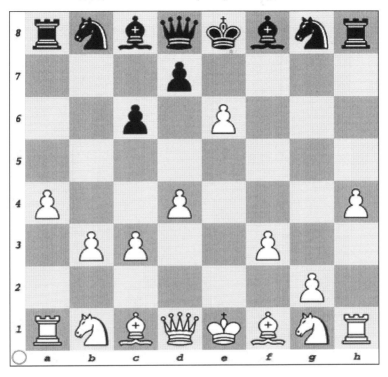

White (Mr. Wills)

Figure 22. "Now, what about the fact that it was my move?" said Mr. Wills.

"It's all about the number of moves each side has played. As Alex said earlier, either black and white have played the same number of moves, in which case it is white to move next, or else white has played one move more than black, in which case it is black's move."

"I understood that from what you said earlier," said Mr. Wills, "but you can't tell how many moves each side has played, not least because pawns can move either one square or two squares on their first move, so once they've reached the fourth rank it's simply not possible to know exactly how many moves they've made!"

Alvaston was silent for a bit, as if uncertain as to what to say, which was most unlike him. Looking back, the reason was Mr. Wills blunt statement that the puzzle was impossible to solve. If I had said that I would be treated to an equally blunt riposte, but Parkes' natural politeness forbade him from flatly contradicting his teacher. In the event he ignored the statement and pressed ahead with his explanation.

"Let's start with white. How many moves has white made?"

Mr. Wills and I started counting, but we were both beaten by Alex. "Nine," he said, "if the ones furthest down the board all moved two squares on their first move. Thirteen if they all moved only one square, or if some of them moved two and some one you could get any number in between."

"Correct!" said Parkes. "But did you consider that some of the moves might have been captures?"

Alex thought for an instant, then replied "It doesn't make any difference. Whether you move a pawn normally or make a capture you still move one square up the board."

"A budding champion and a budding logician – excellent!" Alvaston was getting excited. "So white has made between nine and thirteen moves, but how many moves has black made?"

I studied the board along with the others, but none of us could make any progress.

"The first key is to note that all of white's pieces are still on the board."

"Why is that important?" I asked.

"Because pawns can only change file if they make a capture, which means that the six black pawns no longer on the board were all captured on their own files."

"So what?"

"Well take black's h pawn, for example. On which square was it captured?"

I looked back at the position. "It must have been captured on h4," I replied.

"Exactly," said Parkes. "It was captured on h4. But that means that the pawn currently on h4 must have come from g3."

"And it can only have got to g3 by capturing black's g pawn!" I added, catching some of the excitement. "So that's five moves, if they both moved two squares on their first move, otherwise it's six or seven moves."

"That's right," Alvaston confirmed, "and you can use the same logic for black's a and b pawns, although it is also possible in this case that black's a pawn was captured on a3 and black's b pawn on b3, which would entail an extra move. Hence black's a and b pawns must have made between five and eight moves between them."

"Wait a minute," I interjected, "couldn't black's g pawn have been taken on g4 by the pawn on e6?"

"Excellent observation, Robert. That's really good thinking, but in fact it couldn't have happened, because the pawn on e6 has to have come either from e2 or f2. If it came from e2, capturing on g4 on the way, it must also have captured on f3, f5 and e6 as well, which is four captures, but only three black pawns are missing from these files. If, on the other hand, it came from f2 it made three captures, but now the pawn from e2 must also have made a capture as it now sits on f3, so again one too many captures."

"That means black's a, b, g and h pawns made in total between ten and fifteen moves," said Mr. Wills. I think I can see where this is going."

"Then would you like to finish the explanation Mr. Wills?" Parkes asked.

"OK I'll give it a go. Black's e and f pawns are only significant in that they clearly weren't captured on their starting squares, because the white pawn that captured them would still be there." He looked up for confirmation and saw Parkes nodding with a smile. "So," Mr. Wills continued, "the *minimum* number of moves black can have made is thirteen, five for the a and b pawns, five for the g and h pawns and one each for the c, e and f pawns."

"And the *maximum* number of moves white can have made is also thirteen," said Alex.

"And black can't have made more moves than white," Mr. Wills continued, "which can only mean that both sides must have made exactly thirteen moves."

"Which in turn means that it has to be white's move next. Perfect!" exclaimed Parkes. "Well done everyone!"

The rest of us stayed silent for several seconds, contemplating the astonishing train of thought that had led to Parkes' remarkable conclusion. We might have stayed longer, but as if on cue the bell rang for the start of afternoon school.

***

It turned out I was completely wrong about the message Alvaston sent to Sophy. The following Sunday he passed his phone across to me after lunch. Sophy had texted a reply: IT'S YOUR MOVE. Even then I wasn't sure that she'd understood the message, but Alvaston was utterly convinced that she had understood everything. "I'll phone her back tonight," he determined, "and invite her out on a date! Where do you think I should take her, Robert? What about chess club in town – they meet on Wednesday nights, if I'm not mistaken."

We spent many hours that evening discussing what would and would not be appropriately romantic for a first date.

I don't know what type of date Alvaston settled on, but in the event it didn't make any difference, because the following day was the Monday on which the lockdown was announced. Cinemas were shut, restaurants were shut. Even school was closed, and we weren't even allowed out of the house except to exercise, on our own, for one hour a day.

So Alvaston's first date was put on hold. He did phone her, nevertheless. I have no idea how the conversation went, but their on-line relationship blossomed into a series of video calls. At any time of day or night Alvaston would be prone to shut himself in his room to whisper sweet nothings to his beloved... or maybe to discuss chess problems?... I have no idea what they talked about.

The thing was, though, there was no school (or precious little, just the odd on-line session and some light homework), and I couldn't get out. Alvaston kept disappearing to talk with his new girlfriend and I quickly became bored.

My ennui lasted for exactly five days, until the Friday evening. We were eating dinner when Alvaston's phone buzzed in his pocket. He looked at the screen and said, "Please may I take this – it's my Dad – he wants me to set up a zoom call on my laptop."

"Yes of course," said Dad. "Send him our regards."

"And tell him we're keeping you well fed!" added Mum.

"Robert, would you like to come and meet my dad?"

"Yes, of course." He had told me a lot about his dad, and it was going to be interesting to meet him. I followed Alvaston to his room, where he repositioned his laptop to capture both of us, me in the easy chair while Parkes sat on the edge of his bed.

The screen buzzed, and Alvaston's dad appeared. He was thin-faced, like Alvaston, and had a similarly crooked nose. Unlike Alvaston, however, he was completely bald.

"Who's that?" asked his dad. There was no 'Hello!' or 'How are you, son, I haven't seen you in a long time.'

"This is Robert – the friend I'm staying with."

"Do you trust him?"

"Yes. Absolutely."

I wasn't entirely sure I had yet earned that level of trust, but I felt honoured nonetheless. On later reflection it was, much more significantly, a mark of respect of the father for the son that he accepted Alvaston's statement at face value and continued the conversation, especially given what he had to say.

"Thanks for your help with Champion Computers. They've been removed from the competition and everything's been cleared up."

"That's great! Are you back at home now?"

"No – this business in the Middle East is turning out to be much more interesting than I thought. Looks like I'll be stuck here for some time."

"Anything you want me to do while you're away?"

"As a matter of fact there is. I think that Champion Computers have some form. They were implicated in a very old case of mine. We never got to the bottom of it and I'd like you to take a look at it again."

"What was it about?"

"It was in the very early days of chess computers. None of them back then could play anywhere near the level of a human, but Champion was, literally, the champion, in that their computer regularly wiped the board with every opponent. Until one day there was a challenge from a small up-and-coming company called simply "SW1". A match was set up, with the title up for grabs. Both companies lead programmers were there. The match seems to have been set up fairly and Champion were about to lose."

"What happened?"

"There was an explosion. Not a big one but both programmers were killed. SW1, though, was entirely built around this one person and the company quickly fell by the wayside, clearing the way for Champion to dominate the field for many years. Of course we suspected them of causing the explosion, but we couldn't prove anything. I'm sending over the file – everything's in there."

"OK, Dad, I'll look into it." Alvaston said this in a casual manner, as if his dad was reminding him to water the houseplants, but I knew he was excited.

"Oh, and one more thing. I hear you're romantically involved?" How on earth did he find that out from the Middle East?

Alvaston didn't seem at all surprised, though. "Yes, sort of – we're taking it slowly."

"Good. Just, er, just remember that, um, that things don't always turn out the way you want."

I remembered that Alvaston's mum had passed away and wondered whether he was referring to that in some way.

"I know, Dad," he answered softly.

"How's this Robert at retro-analysis?"

"Working hard, but still at pretty elementary level." I couldn't argue, but it was still annoying Alvaston and his dad talking about me as if I wasn't there with them on the call.

"Try him on the affair on the Siberian rail carriage. It probably won't help much in this particular case, but it might help your friend to get to grips with the subject." And with that, he was gone. I hadn't said a word, which was probably just as well as most of the time I didn't have a clue what they were talking about.

Alvaston looked sad for a moment, wishing I think that the call could have been longer. But he brightened up quickly and asked for the third book from the right on the top bookshelf. I passed him "Duffield Parkes" by Jeremy Wiltshire.

"Duffield was my dad's dad – my grandfather," explained Alvaston while thumbing through the pages. "Here we are – The Affair on the Siberian Rail Carriage."

"What on earth was that?" I asked.

"Someone high up in the Russian government, or the Soviet government as it was then, was accused of carrying on an affair with the wife of a British diplomat while riding on the Siberian express, if I remember. The Foreign Office asked my grandfather to look into it. The Russian was indeed carrying on an affair, as it happened, but not with the diplomat's wife."

"But none of that needs to concern us here. My dad was referring to this case, I'm sure, because it all hinged around a very particular chess position." He found the page he was looking for and set up the board.

"The diplomat's wife was in her early fifties at the time. In her younger days she had become quite a well-known player, but her career in that direction was cut short by a riding accident."

"A riding accident?"

"Yes, Robert, a riding accident. Her horse bolted and she was thrown off. She landed on her head, and she wasn't wearing a helmet at the time. It left her with equinophobia – that is fear of horses – to the point that whenever she played chess after the accident she could never even touch a knight, except to take an opponent's knight and remove it from the board. She also had occasional blackouts – these had died away over time but just before this affair blew up they had been coming back. Duffield, so the story goes, smuggled himself onto the train and came across the pair playing chess together. This was the position…"

Black (Russian Official)

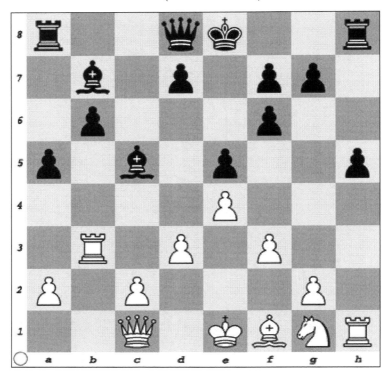

White (British Diplomat's Wife)

Figure 23. Position as observed by Duffield Parkes on the Siberian rail carriage.

"My grandfather confronted her at once, stating for everyone to hear that she had moved a knight. The woman denied it, but couldn't deny the logic that Duffield brought to the case. Under interrogation she confessed that she wasn't, in fact, the diplomat's wife at all! She was a Stasi agent spying for the East Germans – red on red, you might say. When they went back to search her cabin they found the diplomat's wife drugged and asleep. When she awoke she assumed at first that she'd had one of her blackouts – almost the perfect cover for the Stasi agent! Anyway, both the British and the Russian government were enormously grateful – as was the British diplomat, for whom my grandfather had saved both his job and his marriage!"

Of course I borrowed the book and read the story for myself. It is quite incredible how the whole complex web of lies surrounding the Russian official, the diplomat and the Stasi agent could be unravelled just by analysing a single game of chess, and I thoroughly recommend every reader to acquire a copy of that remarkable book.

"Anyway," he added, "Dad thinks that this is a good test for your newfound skills in retrograde analysis. In any case, we can't do anything until we get those files from Dad, so we might as well get stuck in. How did Duffield know that white had moved one of her knights? This one is quite hard, though, so I'll give you a clue – it's all about pawn captures."

Chapter 9. Never Miss a Mate-in-One

Not for the first time since Alvaston arrived I wondered how I could have ended up in this situation. I had missed my tea to meet Alvaston's father, only to find myself now being subjected to an intense examination in high level retrograde analysis.

At the same time, for some reason I couldn't put my finger on, I desperately wanted to pass the exam.

Black (Russian Official)

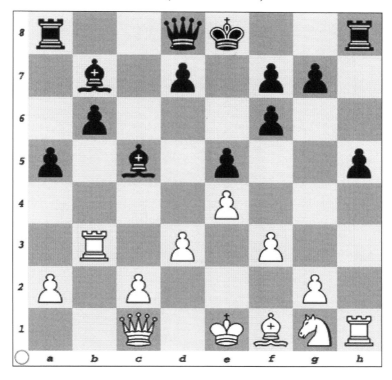

White (British Diplomat's Wife)

Figure 24. How did Duffield know that white had moved one of her knights?

I sat still, as Alvaston had done with Sophy's problem, to carefully consider the position. I started with Alvaston's clue about pawn captures and quickly saw that black's pawn on f6 had to have come from e7, which meant that the pawn on e5 must in fact be black's c pawn. I could account, therefore, for three captures. There were twelve white pieces on the board, which meant that only four were missing: two pawns a bishop and a knight.

The Stasi agent said that she hadn't moved the missing knight, which meant that it had to have been taken on its own square – perhaps by one of the black knights.... I gave myself a kick mentally: I was starting to descend into speculation, which Alvaston considered a capital offence. Nonetheless, if the knight was captured on its own square, then the three captures made by black had to be the two pawns and the bishop. But why couldn't that be the case?

Alvaston Parkes: Chess Detective

After twenty minutes or so I very nearly gave up and asked Parkes for another clue, but something held my attention to the position. Something about *where* the three captures took place, which could only be d6, e5 and f6.

Suddenly, it hit me. The missing white pawns were the b and h pawns, both a long way from the capture positions. To get to the d file the b pawn would have had to make two captures, and even to get to the f file the h pawn would have had to make two captures. That made four captures altogether – but there were only two black pieces missing from the board, so that was impossible! Adrenalin started coursing through my veins, but I forced myself to keep calm and go through my logic carefully before revealing the solution to Alvaston.

I stepped through my reasoning. The b pawn had to get to at least the d file, which involved two captures, right? But what if it had promoted? Then it could have become a queen or a bishop, say (obviously not a knight!) and moved to any of the spaces to be captured. My enthusiasm dropped like a burst balloon.

I could almost hear Alvaston berating me, "You've only scratched the surface, Robert," or something like that. I steeled myself to keep going. Could white have promoted the b pawn without making any captures? No – because the black b pawn can't have changed file without making a *fourth* capture, which would have involved white's knight in one of the captures. Thus the b pawn had to make at least one capture en route to promotion. That only left one capture for the h pawn – too few to reach the capture squares, so it too must have been promoted. But one capture from the h file only gets to the g file, and black's pawn hadn't moved from g7. Maybe that was it.

My excitement was rising again as I carefully stepped through the logic once more. I could see no flaws this time, and proudly announced the result.

"Absolutely first class!" exclaimed Parkes as I finished with my reasoning. "I knew you'd see the first part, that the pawns couldn't have reached the right files through normal captures, but I honestly didn't think you'd consider the possibility of promotion – well done old chap!" He suddenly became sombre and lowered his voice. "Yes, I do believe you're ready, Robert, and it's just as well because I have a feeling that this case will test us both to the absolute limit."

***

The first thing to arrive from Alvaston's Dad the next day was a letter in a white envelope which, surprisingly, was addressed to me. I tore it open to find a small scrap of paper. On it was an eleven-digit number and a hastily written note in small and large letters:

This is my emergency number. DO NOT SHOW IT TO ANYONE except Alvaston. DO NOT PUT IT INTO YOUR PHONE OR ANY OTHER ELECTRONIC DEVICE. Keep it somewhere safe and ONLY USE IT IN AN ABSOLUTE EMERGENCY.

Regards,

Sinfin Parkes

I showed the letter to Alvaston. I thought the note was rather strange, but Alvaston seemed to think it was perfectly normal, although he did seem rather sombre about the whole thing. He suggested that I put it in the "Duffield Parkes" book I had borrowed and was insistent that I go upstairs and hide it before I forgot.

The letter was followed later that morning by two large boxes, each containing a chess computer. Both were newly packaged in cardboard and cellophane, and unopened. One had the Champion emblem, a charging knight, emblazoned across the front. The other had SW1 written in sharp, angular characters. These were presumably the same model as the computers used by the two companies in the match-up, but how Alvaston's dad had managed to obtain pristine, unopened versions was beyond my understanding.

I read from the front of the Champion box "The Champion 5 Chess Computer is the most advanced on the market! With eight playing levels and an opening book stretching to up to 5 moves each, it will be the perfect chess partner whether you are a beginner or a budding world champion. But watch out – the Champion 5 NEVER misses a mate-in-one! With thirty-two high quality plastic pieces…"

"Just go back a bit," said Parkes.

"What – the Champion 5 never misses a mate-in-one?"

"Yes – that's interesting!" interjected Parkes, who was reading the equivalent blurb on the SW1 box. "This one says the same thing… 'SW1 have introduced a new algorithm such that this model never misses a mate-in-one.' That could be helpful to the case!"

"How?" I asked.

"I'll show you later," said Alvaston, "let's open these boxes first and see if the computers are still working. They must be pretty old."

We started with the Champion 5. It was a flattish box about fifteen by fifteen centimetres and three centimetres high, with top of the box doubling as a chessboard. There was a line of red LED lights to the left of the board, one for each row, and another line along the top, one for each column, which we surmised were to inform the user of the computer's chosen move, but no obvious way for the user to communicate their move to the machine. I checked the instructions while Alvaston opened the bag of pieces and set up the board. "The Champion 5 is *sensomatic*," I read. "Just play your moves naturally, making sure you press down on the starting square and again on the square you move to – it's as simple as that!"

Once the board was set up we plugged the machine in. All of the LED lights flashed twice and then went dark.

"Press the white king down twice on its own square," I said, reading from the instructions. "That tells the computer we want to be white." Parkes did so. "Press one of the pawns twice to set the playing level – 'a' pawn is level 1, 'h' pawn is level 8." Parkes pressed the white 'e' pawn twice as instructed. "Now you're ready to start."

We played a game against the computer. In terms of playing strength it was absolutely awful, playing seemingly random and senseless moves – even I could beat it easily, and that was on level 5. We tried again on level 8 with only marginally better results. "This would only be your 'perfect chess partner' if you were a complete beginner!" I said.

"Don't despise small beginnings," said Alvaston. "These were some of the first chess computers ever marketed. Computers are better than humans now, but they had to start somewhere."

We opened the second box. The SW1 machine was somewhat different – it had an array of buttons to input your moves, while a tiny LED screen like the ones you find on really old-fashioned calculators displayed the move to be made by the computer. This machine boasted 'two hundred and fifty-six' playing levels, but even at the top level, playing exceedingly slowly, the moves were just as erratic as with the Champion 5.

We quickly grew bored playing against the machines, and I asked Alvaston to show me what he meant about never missing a mate-in-one and how that could be helpful. He powered down the SW1 machine and drew his own chessboard toward him. "Have a look at this position," he said once he had set up the pieces. "Say black has just moved. Normally of course we would have no way of working out what his last move was. But what if these two computers were playing each other. Then we'd know exactly what black's move was!"

Black (SW1)

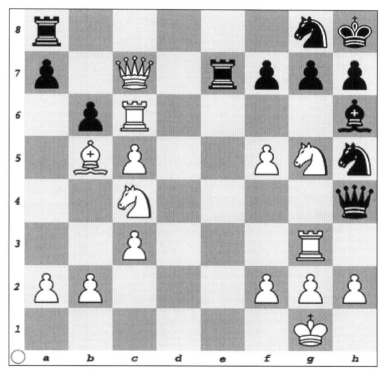

White (Champion 5)

Figure 25. Alvaston's made-up example of a game between Champion 5 and SW1. SW1 has just moved as black: what move did it make?

Chapter 10. Champion Beaten!

"Black is threatening mate in one," I started, "and it never misses a mate-in-one, so white is in trouble."

"Irrelevant." Stated Parkes baldly. "We're interested in what just happened, not what is going to happen – and anyway white can block the mate-in-one pretty easily."

"Not the way these computers play," I joked.

"Please can you try to concentrate on the problem." Parkes was getting a bit uptight.

"OK – well, as you say, normally black has any number of last moves." Quoting Parkes own words seemed like a safe way to start. "But we know that black never misses a mate-in-one, so before his move he can't have been threatening a mate-in-one as he is now."

"You're getting there – keep going."

Black (SW1)

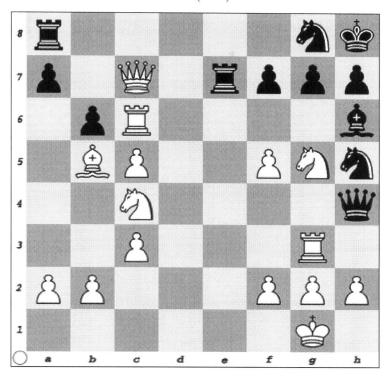

White (Champion 5)

Figure 26. Alvaston's made-up example of a game between Champion 5 and SW1. SW1 has just moved as black: what move did it make?

"So either the rook moved to e7 last turn, or else black moved another piece out of the way of the rook further down the e file. But the only piece that can have moved from the e file is the queen, and if the queen were on e4 it could itself have delivered checkmate. So black's last move was Re7!" I sat back in satisfaction.

"So far so good, Robert, but where did the rook move *from*?"

"Well it can't have moved from anywhere on the e file, because Re1(checkmate) would still be available. Equally, it can't have come from d7 because then Rd1 would be checkmate." I sat for a while longer, but finally shook my head "I'm sorry, Parkes. I just don't see it."

"Don't forget captures, Robert. In retrograde analysis the pieces off the board are just as important as the pieces on it!"

I looked again. "OK, I see – the black rook moved to e7 capturing a white piece on the way."

"Exactly! It must have moved to e7, capturing a white bishop. But where did it move from?"

"How do you know it was a bishop?" I asked.

"Because the black-squared bishop is the only white piece that isn't still on the board."

I felt like an idiot, but I returned my attention to the problem and quickly identified the answer to Alvaston's question.

"For the bishop to have been preventing checkmate the black rook must have come from e8."

"Yes!" said Parkes. "Black's last move can only have been to move the rook from e8 to e7, capturing a white bishop."

I had another question. "I saw you arranging the position around the black king quite carefully – why did you have to hem it in so?"

"That's a good question, Robert. Let's say I'd set up the position like this," and he rearranged the board.

Black (SW1)

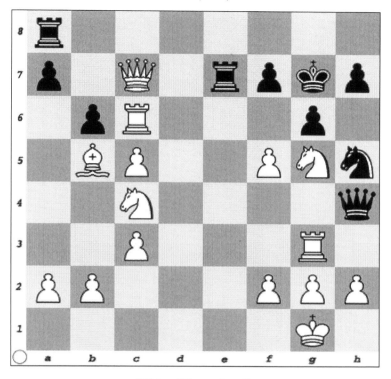

White (Champion 5)

Figure 27. Alvaston's second made-up example of a game between Champion 5 and SW1.

Superficially this problem looks the same, and Rxe7 is still a possible last move, but now there is another possibility, because the black king could have been in check: maybe the white bishop was on g7 and was taken by the black king."

"And if black was in check then he had to get out of check so Re1 is no longer legal," I added, "so it's not a mate-in-one."

***

We had to wait another day for the promised files. I turned back to my homework, which for some reason our teachers still expected us to do, even though we only had a few on-line lessons. Alvaston dismantled and reassembled the computers – I have no idea what he was looking for.

As soon as the files arrived – by courier – we grabbed them and rushed upstairs to Alvaston's bedroom. Alvaston took the police report, along with his dad's copious notes, while I took the press cuttings, and between us we sorted out in outline what had happened.

The competition was held behind closed doors in a hotel room in Kensington. There were five people in the room: the Chief Technical Officer from each of the companies: their job was to operate their computer under the watchful eye of the two referees. The senior referee was Helena Gunther, apparently quite a chess prodigy in her time, although I hadn't heard of her. The junior referee was Jack Lanyard, head of computing at the English Chess Federation. The fifth person in the room was Laura Cummings, a photographer from the Evening Standard.

"There are three photographs taken by the photographer in the police files," said Parkes, passing them across. "The first two are of the competitors shaking hands with the two umpires. The third captures what we think was the final position just before the bomb exploded."

"That's a bit suspicious," I said, taking the photos, "that she took a photo just before it went off."

"Maybe," said Parkes, "but apparently she was taking photos right the way through the match. The files say there are twenty-one pictures, but there are only three in the file. It looks like someone has taken the others out."

The last photo showed two chess computers, identical to the ones we had unwrapped the day before, sitting side by side with the same position on each but with the colours reversed. A hand was caught in the top corner of the photo, suggesting that the two CTOs were sitting side by side behind the two computers.

"According to the press cutting, one of the referees would read the move made by each computer and relay it to the CTOs, who would physically enter the move into their computer and move the pieces appropriately on their respective boards."

Parkes passed another photo across while continuing to read through the police report. "This one captures the scene when the police arrived. Complete mayhem. The two CTOs, the photographer and the junior referee all dead. The senior referee, Helena Gunther, survived because she was taking a bathroom break at the time the bomb went off."

"That sounds suspicious," I said again.

"Please try not to jump to conclusions, Robert. Of course the police looked closely at Miss Gunther, and my father did too, but according to these notes they found nothing linking her to the bomb – in fact rather the reverse."

"What do you mean?"

"The police found a tiny timing mechanism." Parkes passed a fifth photograph across, showing what looked like a tiny electrical component with wires sticking out. "Not small by today's standards but very tiny at the time. The only reason they could think of for making it quite so small was to hide the bomb in one of the pieces."

"That's a very small bomb," I said.

"Yes, but look again at the picture of the aftermath. The blast radius was pretty small – the basic structure of the building is still intact. It's probably only because the room was so small that the poor people in it perished."

"Why does that point away from Miss Gunther?" I asked.

"Because the pieces were brought in by the two CTOs. Each of them brought in a single machine, which had to be straight off the production line and wrapped in its original packaging – not because they were afraid of bombs, of course, but they were each petrified that the other side would cheat by using a much larger computer, or somehow telling the computer which moves to play."

"Which piece was the bomb in?" I asked idly.

"They never found out, but I think that's the key question, Robert."

"You mean if the bomb was in an SW1 piece then they are to blame, but if it was in a Champion piece then they are the culprits."

"Exactly!" said Parkes. "Though probably not the CTOs themselves. In a crime of passion someone might just kill themselves alongside their victim, but this looks more like a case of financial benefit: SW1 went out of business pretty much directly as a result of this event, leaving the field wide open for Champion."

"Couldn't the police work out from this picture where the centre of the blast was?" I asked, holding up the aftermath photo.

Parkes thought about that for a minute. "That's actually a good idea, Robert. They didn't have the technology at the time, but maybe now it might be possible." On the one hand he sounded surprised that I could have any ideas worth pursuing, but on the other hand he immediately took a photo of the photo on his phone and sent it to 'a friend' who happened to be an expert in bomb scene analysis. I wondered, not for the first time, exactly who Alvaston was and whether I was wise to get involved.

It was getting late, and we decided to call it a day in order to make an early start the next morning.

"Are you going to tell Sophy that we're looking into Champion's past?" I asked.

"That's difficult, Robert. On the one hand, I think her analytical skills would be invaluable. On the other, she is herself head of technology acquisition at a competitor company – we have to consider the ethical implications, even though all this is a long time ago."

"Do you trust her to keep it confidential?"

"Yes, of course." Parkes had been seeing her for just over a week, and that through on-line phone and video calls, but he clearly felt he knew her well enough.

"Well tell her, then, but ask her to keep it to herself."

"Just before we wind up," I said, "do we know why they thought this was taken just before the end of the game?" I held up the photo with the position on.

Parkes took the photo. "Champion was black, and it's their move," he said. "You can tell that because the referee moves this flag from right to left depending on whose move it is." He pointed to a tiny pointer, hardly visible in the photograph, which was pointing towards the Champion 5 computer. Then he laid out the position on his own board and looked at it for all of two seconds. "I think it's pretty obvious." He said. "It's mate in one - whatever Champion does, they've lost. But can you prove it?" he asked, looking in my direction.

Alexander G Wilson

Black (Champion 5)

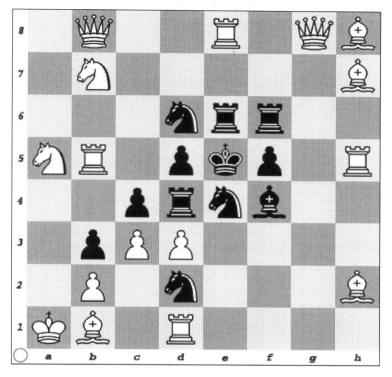

White (SW1)

Figure 28. "It's mate in one – whatever Champion does, they've lost. But can
you prove it?"

Chapter 11. Apocalypse - Pt 1

"How on earth did they get to that position?" I asked.

"You've seen how badly they played when we tried them out yesterday. It is extraordinary, though – at least seven of the pieces are promoted and only one of them promoted to a queen!"

"I can see there are promoted pieces," I said, "but how do you get to seven?"

"That's easy," said Alvaston. "All sixteen of white's pieces are still on the board, so the five missing white pawns have all promoted, and black has an extra knight and an extra rook, so they must also be promotions."

"OK, so at least seven promotions, and on top of that white is threatening checkmate in two, three – no four different ways!"

"Yes, that's interesting," mused Parkes. "But have you confirmed the mate in one yet?"

Alexander G Wilson

Black (Champion 5)

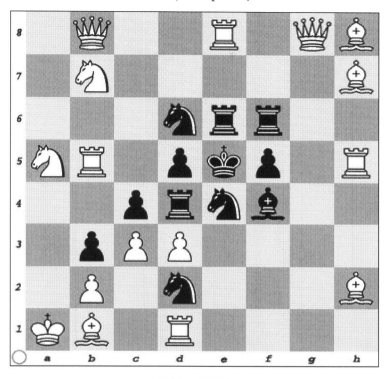

White (SW1)

Figure 29. "It's mate in one – whatever Champion does, they've lost. But can you prove it?"

It took me longer than two seconds, but "Yes," I said eventually. "Most of black's pieces are pinned, so there aren't many to check. He can move his rook on e6, the bishop on f4 or take the pawn on d3 with either the pawn or the rook but in each case Rxf5 is checkmate. If, on the other hand, he moves his knight on e4 to g5 or g3 to cover that threat, then Nc6 is still checkmate for white."

"Quite. And we know that neither side will miss a mate in one, so we can conclude that this photograph was taken exactly one move before the end of the game."

So far so good. I turned in for the night, leaving Alvaston tapping away on his laptop, preparing to bring Sophy up to date with the latest developments.

***

The next morning, bright and early, I was sitting in the easy chair in Alvaston's room. Alvaston was sitting on the bed, and Sophy was smiling out of the laptop on the chest of drawers.

Alvaston took the lead. "I went through the police files again last night, and I found two incredibly valuable pieces of information that we missed," he said. "First of all, the files were meant to include a record of the game, but that has disappeared along with the missing photographs. It seems that someone has gone to great lengths to cover up what happened in the game itself."

I couldn't immediately see how this helped us. "What was the second thing?"

"When the police examined the timer, they found that it was hardwired for exactly five minutes."

"OK – and how does that help us?" I had been hoping for something a bit more tangible.

"Because, Robert, we know that the bomb was primed towards the end of the match, either just before or just after this photograph was taken!" He waved the photo showing the position. "And we know that someone is trying to cover up exactly what happened in the game."

"But we know what happens next," said Sophy from the laptop. "It's mate in one."

"Precisely my point!" Alvaston was full of the chase. "There's no point going to such lengths to hide what's clearly visible to anyone. So if what they're trying to hide is the priming of the bomb, then it must have been sometime in the five minutes immediately before this picture was taken. We're on the move!"

I didn't say anything. Parkes clearly saw this as a great step forwards, but I wasn't sure why. Sophy left her position screenside to get a coffee. Alvaston, meanwhile, started pacing the room, hands behind his back, picking his way carefully between my chair and the dirty clothes spread liberally across the floor.

"Five minutes – at the rate they were playing that's a maximum of five moves; three for white and two for black." He was talking to himself as he paced. "They're hiding something. Something to do with the game itself."

"That's it!" He turned back to me. Sophy had just returned and was warming her hands on a coffee mug. "Something happened *in the game*. Something happened in the last five moves that they, whoever they are, didn't want us to see!"

"But they took the game record. We don't know what those moves were," said Sophy.

"Then we'll work them out. Sophy – have you heard of retrograde analysis?"

"Yes, of course, but it's very unusual for it to be applicable in real life."

"Yes it is, but there are features in this game that make me think it just might be possible. Robert – how many ways is white threatening checkmate?"

"Four, as things stand now."

"But we know that neither computer can have missed a mate-in-one. That must narrow down the possibilities!"

"But what if it was five moves ago, Alvaston?" Sophy was speaking from the laptop screen. "How could anyone possibly work out the last five moves?"

"One by one," he replied.

***

It was over an hour later, and I was the first to give up. "I can't work it out, Alvaston," I said. "White is threatening checkmate all over the place, and I can't find any move that white can have made that he didn't have checkmate as an alternative!"

"Do you remember the trial position I showed you?" asked Parkes. "You asked me why I hemmed the king into the corner?"

I remembered it well. "Ah! I said. White must have been in check!"

"Yes, Robert, and there are only three ways that he can have been in check. Either the king moved from a2 to a1, in which case it was obviously the pawn giving check, or there was a black piece — it would have to be a rook or a queen — on b1 that got taken by the white bishop, or black had a rook or a queen on a5 which was taken by the white knight."

Sophy interrupted, "It's almost eleven o'clock — I have a board meeting I have to go to."

"Do you have to go now? We're just starting to make some progress!" said Parkes plaintively.

"Yes, I do — important decisions to make — some things just can't wait! I should have some time later, though, if you want me to look at one of those moves."

"Good idea!" said Alvaston. "You look at bishop takes rook or queen on b1 - if it is feasible, see if you can work out black's move before that. We'll do the same with the other two possible moves."

"Shall we call again at nine tonight?" I suggested.

It was agreed. Sophy left the call and it was just Alvaston and I in the room.

Black (Champion 5)

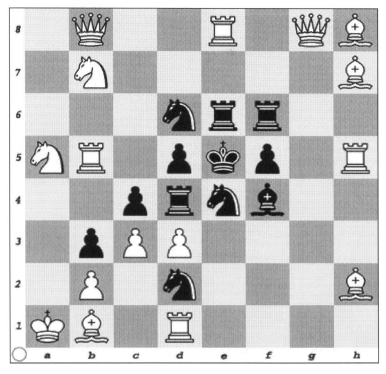

White (SW1)

Figure 30. What was white's last move, and what was black's move before that?

Chapter 12. Apocalypse – Pt 2

Black (Champion 5)

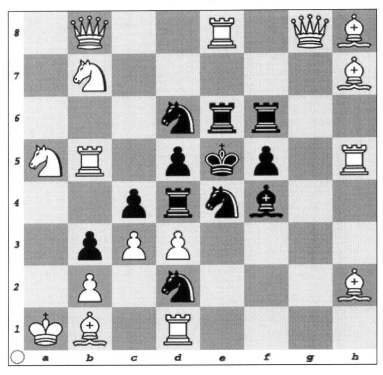

White (SW1)

Figure 31. What was white's last move, and what was black's move before that?

Alvaston and I (Alvaston mainly – but I made the coffee) were ready when the laptop buzzed at nine o'clock that evening and Sophy appeared on the screen.

"You go first," said Alvaston, after the usual ritual of 'Hi's and hand waves.

"Right," said Sophy. "To cut a long story short, it isn't possible that there was a black rook or queen on b1."

"Well done!" said Alvaston, "How did you work that out?"

"Well, first of all, it can't possibly have been a rook, because then the position would have been like this..." she angled her screen so we could see her chess set. It was an unusual set – the pieces were red and blue rather than black and white, and made to look like little soldiers arrayed for battle. This was the position:

Black (Champion 5)

White (SW1)

Figure 32. Previous position if black had a rook on b1.

"I've put the white bishop on c2, but it could be on a2, it makes no difference," she said. "The point is that there's no possible previous move for black – his rook could only have come from c1, and the white king would already be in check, which isn't possible."

"That's clever," I said. "Is it any different with a queen?"

Sophy smiled. "It is the same if the bishop came from c2 – there is no possible previous move for black, but if the white bishop took the queen from a2, then there is a previous move – the black queen could have come from c2."

"So the queen is a possibility then?" I asked.

"No – but you have to go further back to see why." She swapped the pieces round on her board and showed us this position:

Black (Champion 5)

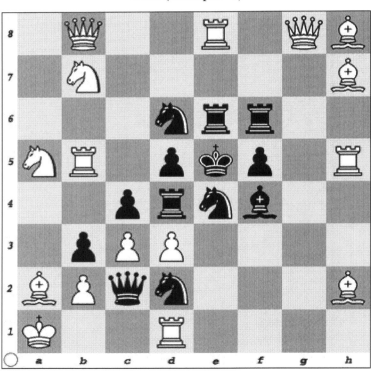

White (SW1)

Figure 33. Previous position if the last moves were Qb1+ followed by Bxb1.

"How do you know that black didn't take something?" I said. "Maybe there should be a white piece on b1?"

"Because," broke in Parkes, "there are sixteen white pieces still on the board, so black clearly hasn't made any captures during the game. Now stop interrupting, old chap, and let Sophy explain."

"Now, " Sophy continued, "applying the same principle as before white must have been in check before his last move, so either the white king has moved from b1 or he was in check from a black piece that he took with his last move with either the rook on d1 or the bishop on a2."

"He couldn't have come from b1," said Parkes, breaking his own rule on interruptions, "because there's no way black could have given check with both his queen and his knight at the same time."

"That's right," said Sophy, "and we can rule out all possible white captures in a single stroke." She looked up from her board and smiled at the camera. Alvaston smiled back, "Yes – clever!"

They were obviously having a moment, and I didn't want to spoil it, but what could I do? "Um, how can we do that, exactly?"

They wrested their attention from each other. "It's all to do with promotions," said Sophy. "White still has sixteen pieces on the board, but only three pawns, so five of white's pieces must be promoted pawns."

"Yes, I can see that." I said.

"But," added Parkes, "since black hasn't made any captures, none of the blacks pawns changed file. So how did the white pawns get past their black counterparts?"

"They must have made captures themselves!" I said.

"Yes," said Sophy, "well, mostly. If the pawn on the h file, say, captured black's g pawn, then both the h and g pawns are free to march on to promotion – so in that case one capture is sufficient for two pawns to promote."

"So the *minimum* number of captures white can have made is three," concluded Parkes. "One to promote his a pawn, a pawn capture to promote his e and f pawns, and another one to promote his g and h pawns."

"And," Sophy added, "with the black queen on the board there are now thirteen black pieces, so all of black's pieces are accounted for."

I must have still looked blank – I could follow the reasoning but I wasn't sure where it was leading. "Look," said Parkes, "those three captures must have occurred *before* white's last promotion, so now, moving backwards through the game, until we get back to sometime before white's last promotion there can never be more than thirteen black pieces on the board."

"And in this line we've already introduced the black queen," said Sophy, "so another capture would leave us with fourteen."

My mind was beginning to ache. It was bad enough with just Parkes, but now they were tag-teaming I was definitely in trouble. I could vaguely see what they meant, though, and working it through in my mind later that evening came to the conclusion that their reasoning was correct.

"So that whole line is impossible," I said at the time, trying to move the conversation on.

"Yes," said Parkes, "white didn't make a capture on b1. That's really good work, Sophy."

Sophy beamed.

"How long have you been playing chess?" I asked.

"I started young." She smiled.

"Did your mum and dad teach you?"

"No, my mother doesn't play, and my father was always at the office. But I had an aunt who was mad keen on chess. We used to play over the web, and when she came to stay we'd play endlessly, or spend our time making up puzzles – but that's a long time ago now."

"Ah – so that's how you got so good!"

"I guess it is. Anyway, how did you two get on with your alternatives?"

"We were looking at the possibilities of the white king moving from a2 to a1, or the knight moving to a5 capturing a queen or a rook," Parkes reminded us. "Robert – do you want to take Sophy through the knight option?"

"Sure," I said, happy to be able to contribute something positive to the conversation. "As Alvaston said, the knight could in theory have moved to a5 capturing a queen or a rook that was checking the white king, but," I paused for dramatic effect, "there is nowhere that the white knight could have moved *from*. All of the squares are occupied apart from c6, and at c6 the knight would have been putting the black king in check, and it can't have been doing that *before* it moved."

"That's good," said Sophy.

"So, having eliminated the impossible," said Parkes, "there is only one remaining move, so that must be the truth: white moved his king from a2 to a1."

"Could he have captured a piece on a1?" asked Sophy.

"I think not," said Parkes, "but I'd like to leave that question for tomorrow. In any case, he moved from a2 to a1, which means we know black's previous move as well: on a2 the king is in check from the black pawn on b3. That pawn can only have come from a4 or b4, and we know that black hasn't made any captures, so black's previous move was pawn from b4 to b3."

We were all excited to have got to this point, but it was past midnight and Alvaston wrapped things up for the day. "We've done really well," he said. "I can't see anything suspicious in these two moves, but we're already 40% of the way to the target. Now we must get some shuteye – it's no use trying to do retrograde analysis when you're half asleep!" He quickly reset our board to the original position and played in reverse the two moves which we had deduced. "Our question for tomorrow is: what was white's last move to reach this position?"

Black (Champion 5)

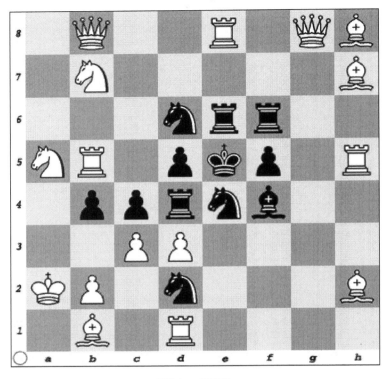

White (SW1)

Figure 34. "What was white's last move to reach this position?"

Chapter 13. Apocalypse – Pt 3

White (SW1)

Figure 35. "What was white's last move to reach this position?"

After a hearty breakfast the next day Alvaston and I retreated to his bedroom and sat in the same formation as before, with Sophy joining us again via the internet.

We studied the position for twenty minutes before anyone spoke.

"Let's start simply," said Alvaston. "The white king must have been in check for the same reason as before, which means there are five possible last moves for white. Let's write them down and see if we can eliminate them one by one as we did yesterday."

I found a pen and some paper. "Well, the king might have moved from a3, b3 or a1," I said, writing those moves down, "unless there is a black piece sitting on a1 – we didn't rule that out yesterday, remember."

"The bishop might have moved from c2 to b1 taking a piece - it would have to be a bishop or a queen to be giving check," said Sophy.

"And the fifth move is the white knight moving to a5 capturing a queen or a rook," finished Parkes.

"I thought we ruled that out yesterday."

"Yes – while the black pawn was on b3 there was nowhere it could have moved from, but now the b3 square is empty we have to consider the possibility that the knight moved from b3 to a5." I wrote it down as the fifth alternative.

"So," I said. "King a3 to a2."

"Impossible," Alvaston said immediately. "On a3 the king is in check from the black pawn on b4, and the pawn has nowhere it could have moved from." I scratched it out.

"And we can rule out b3 as a starting square for the king," said Sophy. "It would be in check from both the knight and the pawn, which is impossible."

"Good!" said Parkes, "we're making progress! What's next on the list?"

"King a1-a2" I answered, "and since white must have been in check, he must have taken a black rook or a black queen."

"Quite right," said Parkes. "It can't have been a rook, because it has nowhere to move from, since we know that black hasn't made any captures, which just leaves the queen."

"The only place the queen could have come from is b3," added Sophy. She swapped a couple of pieces and angled her laptop so we could see her board.

Black (Champion 5)

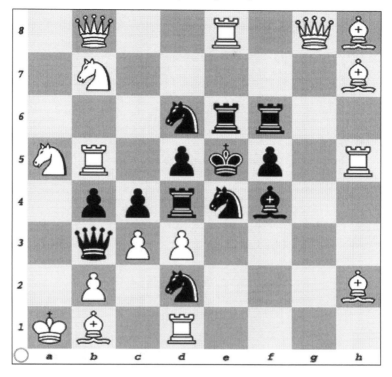

White (SW1)

Figure 36. Position if the next moves were …Qa2+ and Kxa2.

"Before that the white king must have come from a2 again to be in check," she continued, "and now the only place the queen could have come from is c2." She showed us the new position:

Black (Champion 5)

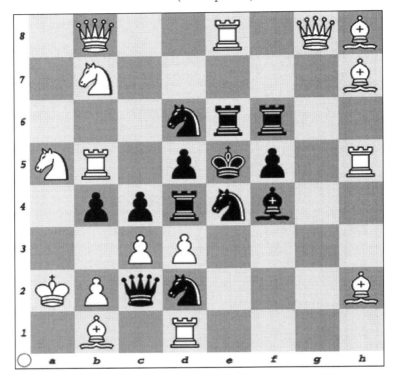

White (SW1)

Figure 37. Position if the next moves were Qb3+, Ka1, Qa2+ and Kxa2.

We looked at this position for a while.

"Once again there are thirteen black pieces on the board," said Parkes finally, "so white's previous move can't have involved a capture. That means the white king must have moved from a3 or b3, but both of those are impossible for the same reasons we discussed yesterday: on a3 white would be in check from the pawn on b4, but there's nowhere that pawn could have moved from to deliver the check, and on b3 white would be in check from the pawn on c4 and the knight on d2 as well as the queen on c2, which again is impossible."

"So that's it then. Three down, two to go," I said, crossing out king a1-a2. "Next is bishop from c2 to b1, taking a bishop or a queen." I reset the pieces on our board to the position at the start of the day and put the white bishop on c2. "It can't have been a bishop," I added, "because there is no square it could have come from to deliver check. So it must have been a queen." I put a black queen on b1.

Black (Champion 5)

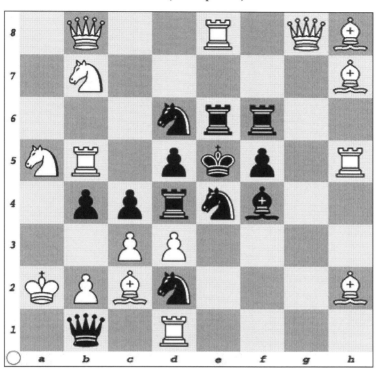

White (SW1)

Figure 38. Position if the next move was Bxb1.

"You're getting the hang of this, aren't you?" said Alvaston, pleased, "so where did the queen come from?"

"It must have come from c1," I said.

"So with the queen on c1," said Parkes, "how can the king have been in check previously, given that there are now thirteen black pieces on the board so white's last move can't have involved a capture?"

"The king must have moved from a3, b3, a1 or b1," I said. "I guess a3 and b3 are out for the same reason as last time... and a1 and b1 are both out because there's nowhere the black queen could have moved from except c1, and the white king would already have been in check!"

"Perfect!" said Alvaston. "Excellent analysis!" It was my turn to beam. Sophy too was smiling through the computer screen.

"So," continued Parkes, "the only remaining move for white – and hence the one he played – is knight from b3 capturing a queen or a rook on a5."

"It obviously can't have been a rook," said Sophy, "because it can't have come from anywhere which wasn't already putting the white king in check."

"Good!" said Alvaston, almost shouting with excitement. "We have another move!"

"But what about the possibility that there was a black piece on a1?" I complained.

"Good point, Robert. It's important to be thorough. I could dimly see yesterday that something like this might be the way forward, which is why I wanted to delay the question. The fact is that an extra black piece on a1 doesn't materially change the analysis – we still get to the same point where white captures a queen on a5, but if there were a black piece on a1 that would make fourteen black pieces on the board, which is too many."

"Let's take a coffee break before we consider black's last move – would you do the honours, Robert? I'll set up the new position."

Black (Champion 5)

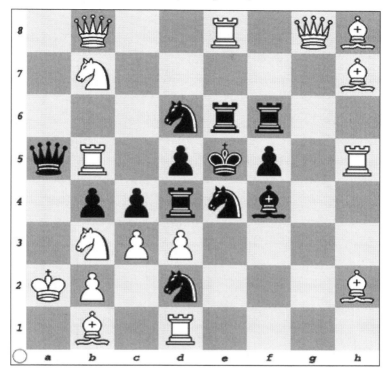

White (SW1)

Figure 39. Position before Nxa5 b3+, Ka1.

"Now," said Alvaston when we were settled again. "There's no possibility of it being a discovered check, so the queen must have moved from somewhere, but where?"

"It can't have moved from a3 or a4 because the king would already be in check," said Sophy through the computer screen, "and we know that black hasn't taken any white pieces, so the queen can't either have come from further up the a file."

"So much is clear," said Alvaston, "so it must have come from b6, c7 or d8, but which one?"

I had a lingering thought in the back of my mind, and after a quarter of an hour of silence I gave it utterance. "We know that white must have been in check before *his* last move, but the only check I can see with the queen on any of those squares is if the king moved from a3, and we know that isn't possible because the pawn has nowhere to move from."

"Quite right," said Parkes distractedly, his mind still on the problem. "We're in a different phase of the problem now."

"What do you mean, 'a different phase of the problem'?"

Parkes stirred himself to give me his full attention. "Up until this point, while the play was at the bottom end of the board, white had to be constantly in check, otherwise he would have missed a mate-in-one, which he never does because 'he' is a computer. Now, however, black has a queen right in amongst it – perhaps the queen can cover enough of the checkmates so that when we reverse white's previous move there are no mate-in-ones for white to miss!"

"So we want to move the queen to a position where it covers the most mate-in-ones?"

"Yes, probably, but better to start with the least likely and try to eliminate it."

"Alright, said Sophy, let's put the queen on d8. That doesn't cover any of the mating threats." She moved the pieces on her board. "White is still threatening mate with his rook or queen on e6 or the rook on f5. The two knight checks on the other side of the board are no longer possible as the knight is now on b3, but that gives an additional mating threat in cxd4."

"That's it!" cried Alvaston. "Given that white wasn't himself in check, that last move cxd4 would always be available to white, and it would always have been checkmate, unless white's last move were with either the knight on b3 or the pawn on c3. But if either of those were white's last move then Rxe6, or indeed one of the other possibilities on that side of the board, would have been a mate-in-one. It's as simple as that!"

"But white could have taken a black piece which was defending the d4 square," said Sophy, "like a rook on d3 for example."

"That's not possible anymore, because black is up to his full complement of thirteen pieces," replied Parkes. "No, the queen can't have come from d8, and exactly the same reasoning applies to c7."

"So the queen came from b6," I said, "but isn't the situation exactly the same?"

"Not quite," said Parkes. "From b6 the queen is covering the d4 square, so cxd4 is no longer a mate in one."

***

We were in the middle of congratulating ourselves on our latest advance when a formally dressed man I didn't recognise appeared behind Sophy and whispered something to her that the microphone didn't pick up. She looked upset. "Sorry – I have to go now. Something's come up," she said.

"Is there anything…" Alvaston started to speak, but Sophy had already left and the screen was black.

"I wonder what that was about," I said. "I hope it wasn't anything too serious."

Alvaston said nothing, but I could tell he was as concerned as I was. Then he shook himself and looked back to the chessboard. "Let's see if we can solve this thing before she comes back. We've only got one more move to work out." He swapped a couple of pieces. "Here's the position. What was white's last move?"

Black (Champion 5)

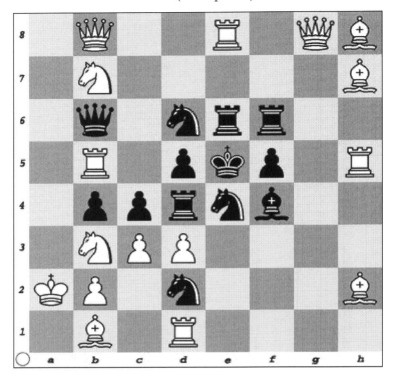

White (SW1)

Figure 40. Position before ...Qa5+, Nxa5 b3+, Ka1. What was white's last move?

But before we could get to grips with it, Mum called from downstairs. It was time for an on-line physics lesson, for both of us, and after tea we were 'all going to watch a film together – anything to get you away from those computer screens'. If only she knew.

Chapter 14. The Best Move

Black (Champion 5)

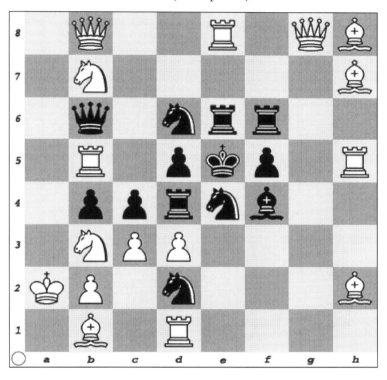

White (SW1)

Figure 41. Position before ...Qa5+, Nxa5 b3+, Ka1. What was white's last move?

We went online at nine o'clock the next morning as usual but Sophy didn't join the call. We still set up the position and stared at it, but it was hard for either of us to concentrate, knowing that Sophy was upset and not knowing why.

"Look," said Parkes finally, "it can't be that hard. White wasn't in check so we're looking for a move before which none of the mate-in-ones existed."

"Well cxd4 is no longer mate-in-one because of the queen," I said, recapping the previous day's work. "That only leaves Rxe6, Qxe6 and Rxf5."

We sat in silence again.

"I don't get it," I said finally. "The mate on e6 is supported by the rook on e8 and the queen on g8, whilst the mate on f5 is supported by the bishop on h7 and the rook on h5 – two totally different sets of pieces. White can't have moved two pieces, and the only way that one of those four can block the other threat is queen to g6 or g5, but in both of those cases Qf5 is checkmate, so it's still mate-in-one."

"That's good analysis, Robert, and I'm right there with you – none of those pieces can have moved. There must be something else."

After a good five minutes Alvaston spoke again, this time with rising excitement. "Yes! The key is the defenders. The knight on d6 would be defending f5 if it weren't pinned by the queen, but it isn't defending the e6 square. The only piece with the potential to defend both e6 and f5 is the rook on f6."

"But that rook is pinned by the bishop on h8," I objected, "and the bishop can only have moved from g7, in which case it was still pinning the black rook."

"Unless it was a pawn at the time," said Parkes.

"Ah, I see – a white pawn on g7 took something on h8 and promoted to a bishop!"

"Actually no, that's not possible, I was just pointing out the possibility." I hated it when he did that – I was just getting excited.

"That's not possible," he continued, "because black has thirteen pieces on the board, remember, so we need a pawn capture, not a piece capture, on the a or b file to get both pawns promoted. But maybe something moved out of the way of the bishop?"

"The only piece that can have done that is the queen on b8, and if that were on b7 the rook would still be pinned by the queen."

"Unless it was a pawn at the time," Alvaston said again.

"So a pawn on g7 moved to g8 and promoted to a queen?" I was more hesitant this time.

"Exactly, Robert, exactly! That's the *only* move that doesn't mean white missed a mate in one. We've cracked the problem, Robert! And I think we might have cracked the case!"

By 'the case' Alvaston was referring to the bomb at the chess competition that had set us off on the quest in the first place. It was clear that Alvaston saw our analysis as immensely significant, but I couldn't see that it had any bearing on the case whatsoever. I was about to ask Alvaston for his thoughts when the computer screen buzzed. Alvaston tapped a few buttons and a woman's face appeared – she was about fifty with blonde hair curling in all directions.

"Dr. Maynard," said Parkes, "Thank you for getting back to me. This is Robert Graham." He pointed in my direction. "It was his idea to ask for your help on this one." Turning to me he added "Dr. Maynard is a forensic scientist – she spends most of her time working with the terror unit on explosions."

"Is he cleared?" asked Dr. Maynard.

"I'd trust him with my life," said Alvaston, and for some reason that seemed to be enough to satisfy her.

"Well," said Dr. Maynard, "we've analysed the photograph you sent us, and from the position of the debris we think we can trace it back to determine which piece the bomb was hidden in."

"Was it the white queen on g8?" said Parkes.

Dr. Maynard looked a bit crestfallen, then in turn a bit annoyed. "If you already knew that, why did you ask me to help?"

"Sorry, Dr. Maynard, we didn't know that before, in fact we only worked it out a few minutes ago – and even then we weren't certain – just a hunch really… but now you've confirmed it I think we're very close to cracking the case. I can't say anything more yet, but when it's all done and dusted I'll bring you up to date – or maybe Dad will – it's his case really."

"And how is your Dad?"

"He's fine – called about a week ago in fact."

Dr. Maynard turned all motherly. "Don't worry – he'll be home soon!"

"I'm sure he will. Thank you again, Dr. Maynard!" and Alvaston closed the call.

I wanted to ask how he knew someone working with 'the terror unit', whatever that was, but I also wanted to know how he knew where the bomb was hidden. The immediate question won out. "How on earth did you know the bomb was in the white queen?" I asked.

"Make a list of the last five moves," he said, so I wrote them down in the order we discovered them: ka1 b3+ Nxa5 Qa5+ g8(Q).

"Now," he continued, "we know that someone was hiding these moves from us, likely because he or she didn't want us to know where the bomb was hidden."

"Yes," I said.

"What marks out the last move as significant?"

"Well it involves a promotion," I said.

"Exactly! The introduction of a new piece – or in this case a bomb – onto the board!"

"But there have already been lots of promotions on both sides. Why would anyone wait until this point in the game to introduce the bomb? Another move or two and the game would have been over."

"Because the other pawns were all underpromoted! You can't suddenly create a piece with a bomb in it. No, you have to create the piece first, and obviously you make it a queen, because who ever promotes to a bishop or a rook?" We both laughed at that. "Imagine their frustration," Parkes continued, "watching these computers play their idiotic moves, watching piece after piece get promoted but none to a queen! But then, just at the last," his face grew suddenly sombre, "the opportunity presented itself."

"But still," I said, "how did you know that it had to be in a promoted piece?"

"Mainly the fact that someone had tried so hard to keep these moves from us, but also… pass me that box will you?" I passed him the box that the Champion computer had come in. "Here we go," he continued, "'With thirty-two high quality plastic pieces…' – you read it out earlier."

"I don't see the point."

"Both sides came prepared with their own computer and pieces – but only thirty-two pieces. Any promoted pieces…"

"must have been supplied by the referee!" I interjected, "– the one who survived because of a fortunately timed bathroom break! That's brilliant, Alvaston!"

***

After a quick lunch Parkes pulled out his father's case notes and started to read about the mysterious Helena Gunther who was refereeing the match. I was put to work on his laptop trying to find out as much as I could from the public record. Every now and then one of us would call out some relevant fact like "She was twenty-six at the time of the match," or "She was under 18 champion when she was only fourteen."

Over time, though, we got more and more frustrated. We had a reasonable profile of her junior chess career, a few tournament results during her years as a young adult, a few stories about the computer competition and the bomb, of course, and then nothing more.

"There's simply nothing there, Alvaston," I complained. "I've tried every combination of 'Helena', 'Gunther', 'chess', 'referee', even 'bomb' but there's simply nothing there."

"I'm not doing any better," said Parkes. "My father looked into her background and it seems that, world-beating chess prodigy apart, she led a fairly normal, uneventful life. Nothing to point to her being a homicidal maniac, anyway."

We took a break, and then hit the internet again. I looked at the database of the English Chess Federation, while Alvaston entered a string of passwords to gain access to his father's on-line files. Neither yielded any new information.

"Of course, there is one reason why Helena Gunther might have dropped out of the records," Alvaston mused.

"What's that?"

"She might have changed her name – she might have got married, for instance."

"I suppose you're right, but if we don't know what she changed her name to it's going to be just as difficult to find her."

"Yes but... I wonder, though. Have a look at this." He pushed the laptop out of the way and, pulling the chessboard towards him, set up a new position.

"Where's this position from?"

"I saw it at Sophy's house."

"What? You've been to Sophy's house?"

"Yes. It's very grand, with big gardens."

"But we're meant to be in lockdown!"

"That's why I went secretly."

"You can't do that! We're meant to be staying at home to save lives! The Prime Minister himself told us to stay apart – or did he give you special permission to break the lockdown because you're Alvaston Parkes?"

"No of course he didn't! The Home Secretary makes those decisions. Manilla envelope, top shelf, sandwiched between the book on the Ruy Lopez and the one on Rigor Mortis."

I gave him some more of my mind as I reached out for the envelope. "Even if he did, that's for serious stuff, not just so you can visit your new girlfriend!" I opened the envelope. It was empty.

"Humbug!" roared Alvaston, "I was hoping you wouldn't have the nous to check!"

We both laughed.

"Seriously, though, did you go to her house?"

"I did – just once, though. You remember her aunt, the one who was mad keen on chess? Well Sophy told me that her aunt proposed to her uncle by giving him a chess problem. Sophy liked the problem so much that her aunt gave her a little ornament – a tiny chessboard with this position on, and the words underneath: 'You're playing white: what's your best move?'"

"OK, but what's that got to do with the case?"

"Nothing, I expect, but you never know — and we could do with a break anyway so let's give it a go, shall we?"

Black

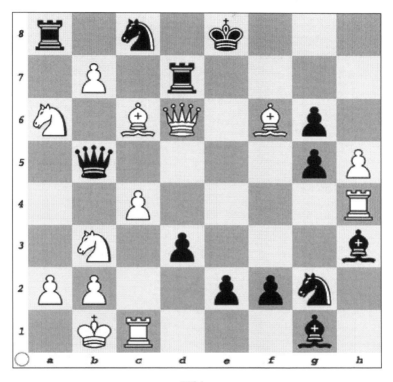

White

Figure 42. "You're playing white: what's your best move?"

Chapter 15. Who Wins?

Black

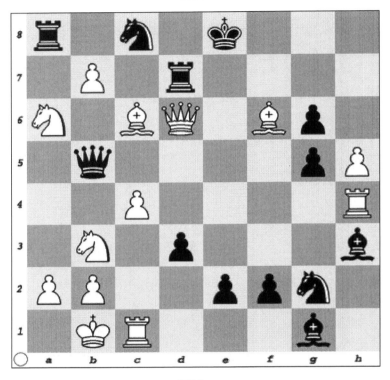

White

Figure 43. "You're playing white: what's your best move?"

"What a strange position," I said. "There are so many good moves."

"Quite so," said Alvaston, "five of black's major pieces are under threat, including the queen from two different directions. But the question is which one is the *best* move?"

"I would think bishop c6 takes queen b5," I put forward.

"But then the black knight takes white's queen, or one of the black pawns queens."

"Alright then, bxa8, promoting to a queen. That pins the knight and threatens to take it next move."

"That's better," said Alvaston, "but is it *the* best? Does it lead to checkmate? In a position like this, with so many pieces en prise, surely a move that was demonstrably the best would have to lead to checkmate."

"It probably does. If black doesn't do anything about it the new queen will take the knight on c8 and after the king is forced to f7 Qa8-f8 is checkmate."

"If black doesn't do anything about it, but he has a number of delaying moves at least. No, let's take a more strategic approach – how can white get the black king in checkmate?"

I studied the position a while longer. "Well the queen can't give check, except on squares where she herself can be taken."

"No," said Parkes, "that's right."

"Which leaves rook e4 (check), but after Kf7 it's hard to see how white can finish it off."

"Or?"

"Or Nc7 (check)! The rook can't take it, and it forks the king and queen!"

"That's all well and good, Robert, but does it lead to checkmate?"

"Well, the king moves to f7 again, and it's not obvious how to get at the king once it has moved to f7."

"Absolutely brilliant, Robert! That's it!"

"What's it?"

"f7. 'It's not obvious how to get at the king once it has moved to f7.'"

"So?"

"So white has to prevent the king from moving to f7. White's best move is to take the pawn on g6, so the king can't move to f7!"

"But that's not even check! Black can make any move he wants."

"True, but he can no longer move his king, and white has a dual threat."

"I can see that Rh8 is checkmate, but black can take the rook with his knight."

"Yes, but then the other threat kicks in, which is to move his knight to c7, which is also checkmate because the black rook is still pinned."

I looked at the position for a while longer. "You're right, Alvaston. It's mate in two."

"And as a simple glance will tell you, there is no mate in one, so this must be white's best move!"

"Clever! Who would have thought it would be a simple pawn move?"

"And beautiful, I think, as a proposal. Sophy's aunt is saying that she knows her future husband has many grandiose options to choose from, but all the time there is a quiet move in the corner which will turn out to be the best."

***

"So – does this have any bearing on the case?"

Alvaston grew suddenly sombre. "I'm afraid it does, Robert, and it means that Sophy might be in grave danger. What was the 'best move'?"

"Why h5 takes g6," I said.

"And how would you write that down, in normal shorthand notation?"

"hg?"

"Precisely!"

"hg – Helena Gunther?"

"I think so, yes. After all it is a proposal – his best move is Helena Gunther. Now if she is indeed Sophy's aunt she would have changed her name to Tarin. Add that to your search and see if it yields anything."

I did so and found just a single hit. A tiny paragraph in the marriages column of a local paper: 'Dr. and Mrs. Gunther are pleased to announce the marriage of their daughter, Helena Gunther, to Mr. Daniel Tarin of Uxbridge.'

I read it out. "If they're a rich family I wonder why they didn't announce it in the Times?"

"First of all, they weren't so rich back then. Secondly, I think they didn't want to make a splash. This announcement, you'll note, comes from Helena's family."

"OK – so it looks like Helena Gunther is Sophy's aunt, but why do you think Sophy is in danger?"

"Because she must know that her aunt is the woman we're looking for – she's not stupid!"

"Why didn't she tell us then?"

"Because she's being coerced into silence. Someone in the household – maybe that man who we saw talking to her – knows what we're doing and is forcing her to keep quiet."

"Or else she's protecting her aunt. She's obviously very fond of her."

"Yes, I suppose that is possible," said Parkes, "though I think I know her better than that."

We parted company for a half hour. Parkes phoned a police contact, someone who knew his father no doubt. I continued to trawl the internet with more combinations of Gunther, Tarin, chess etc. It was when I put in 'Tarin nee Gunther' that I found another small article from a different local newspaper: 'The cause of the crash is not yet certain, but the police believe the brake system may have failed. The only casualty was the elderly driver, Mrs. Helena Tarin nee Gunther.' I ran to tell Alvaston.

"What's the date of the story?" was his immediate question. I had to run back to my room to get the laptop.

"It was the twenty-third of March this year." I checked the date on my phone. "But that's only two days ago!"

"Clever!" said Parkes, "Fiendishly clever. They knew we were getting close so they took her out. But Sophy knows the truth, and that puts her in grave danger."

"Why would they do that, doesn't it make it look even more likely that she was guilty?"

"Look at it his way, Robert, if you were the chief constable, would you reopen a case from the 1970s if you knew that the likely culprit was already dead?"

"Alvaston," I said, changing tack, "I know this is difficult, but have you considered that Sophy might be in on it too?"

Alvaston gave me such a painful, withering stare I wished I could have evaporated on the spot. "No," was all he said. "I don't think so. But we need to find out what she knows, and do it in a way that keeps her safe."

"How can we do that?" I asked.

"I've already done it," said Parkes. I've sent her a coded message in the form of a chess problem. He pulled the board towards him and set the pieces in position. It's black to move, Robert, and the question is simply 'Who wins?' Before you try it, I should warn you that there is no solution, unless you know what happened in the past – which is, of course, the point of the message. I'm asking her to tell me what happened in the past so we can work out together how to move forward."

Black

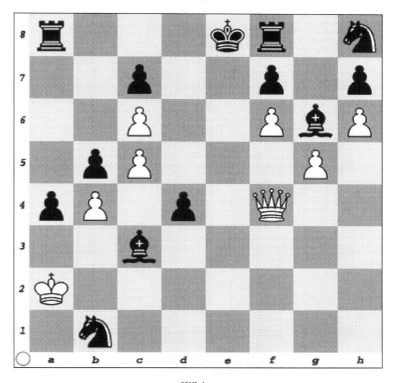

White

Figure 44. "It's black to move, Robert. Who wins?"

Chapter 16. The Password

Black

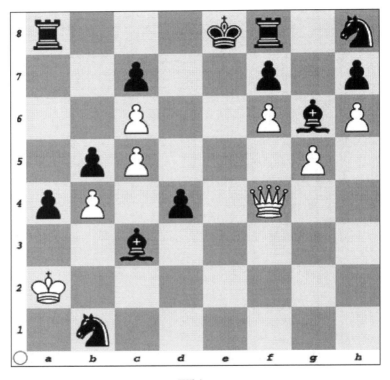

White

Figure 45. "It's black to move, Robert. Who wins?"

Despite the grave circumstances Alvaston was right – we did need a break, and I was intrigued by this particular problem.

"Well, the position of the black king and rook suggest this is a 'can't castle' type of problem." I looked at Alvaston for confirmation, but he stayed silent, staring absent-mindedly at the board.

"If black can castle, his king is safe, and he's a lot of material up, so I guess he'll win." Alvaston stirred – I could see he was gearing up for another of his diatribes about 'proving not guessing', so I quickly nipped it in the bud by adding "but of course we'll have to prove that later." Alvaston sat back again.

"Now if black can't castle, what's the threat? Oh yes – Qe5(check). Is it OK if I move the pieces around?"

"Yes, of course, I remember the position."

I put the queen on e5, moved the king to its only flight square on d8, then moved the queen to e7(check). The king had to move to c8 and then Qxf8 was checkmate. "I've found the threat, but it's black's move, so let's see what he can do about it." I shifted the pieces back to their original positions.

After another five minutes I was ready with my solution. "If black can't castle he has no defence to white's threat," I said. "He can try d3 to cover e5 with his bishop, but Qe3 (check) is then just as powerful. He can try Rg8 but then Qxc7 wins next move, either through Qe7 (checkmate) or if black follows up with Rh7 then Qc8 is checkmate. Finally, white can move his bishop to f5 but white takes it with his queen and the combined threat of Qe5 and Qd7 can't be stopped."

Parkes broke in. "So far, so good, but did you consider Kd8 as black's first move?"

I hadn't, and it cost me another ten minutes of effort. Finally, I came up with Qg4.

"Perfect!" roared Parkes. "After Kd8 Qg4 black has no defence against Qd7 – he can delay it by Bf5, but then it's checkmate next move! Well done, Robert."

"So that's it – if black can't castle white gets checkmate, but if he can castle he wins on material. I must say though, Alvaston," I was treading as carefully as I could, knowing Alvaston's frame of mind, "I don't think this one's quite up to your usual standard. If I can solve it this easily Sophy will surely eat it for breakfast!"

Alvaston threw his head back and laughed out loud. "That would indeed be the case, Robert, if you had actually solved it!"

"But I've shown that white wins if black can't castle."

"Yes."

"And if black can castle his king's safe, and he's lots of material up – OK I haven't *proved* that black can win, but it's pretty obvious!"

"I should like to see you try," said Alvaston, "but I fear it would be too painful for both of us, so I'll simply tell you that it's not true! If black castles white can still force a draw."

I reset the original position and castled for black. "How can that be?" I asked in exasperation. "White's only safe check is Qg4, and after kb8 there are no more checks, so surely black can win from there."

Black

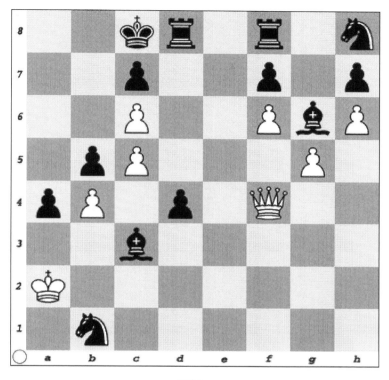

White

Figure 46. "If black castles white can still force a draw."

"In fact there are a couple of moves that draw for white, and Qg4 is one of them."

I raised my eyebrows.

"But the simplest one," he continued, "is Qxc7(check)."

Having been handed the answer it took me only a few seconds to realise that black has to play Kxc7 after which white is in stalemate. "Clever, I suppose," I said begrudgingly. "So if black can't castle white wins, and if he can castle it's a draw."

"Not too bad, but you've missed the 'piece de resistance'."

"And what's that?" I asked.

"Black has a win too. Go back to the original position."

I moved the black king and rook back to their starting squares.

"That's it. Black has a mate in two."

"But if black castles we've shown it's a draw and if black can castle we've shown that white wins."

"Yes, except we missed one potential move when we were considering the alternatives. A move that's regularly missed by players of all standards up and down the country."

"En passant! If white's last move was b2-b4, black can take the white b pawn by moving his a pawn to b3, giving check to the white king, so that white doesn't have time to pursue his own attack!"

"And then?"

"Well the black king has to take back on b3, and then…" I thought for a few more seconds, "… and then Ra3 is checkmate! So all three outcomes are possible, a white win, a black win or a draw, but you can only tell what the outcome will be if you know what happened previously in the game. I take it all back, Alvaston. That is brilliant!"

Alvaston smiled briefly, but before long resumed his concerned expression. He was clearly thinking about Sophy.

"I'm sure Sophy will understand your message." I tried to sound confident. In truth it seemed unlikely, but I had been wrong on that point before. I decided to move the conversation away from Sophy and back onto the case in general. "By the way, what made you think that Helena might be Sophy's aunt?" I asked. "Surely it wasn't a random guess that you suggested we tackle that problem?"

"No, it wasn't random. It's a question of motive. I simply asked myself who had most to gain from killing off the top brains in Champion and SW1."

"And you came up with Helena Gunther?"

"No! I came up with Tarin electronics. When SW1 went under and Champion were knocked back for a while, who came charging up on the fence to compete with Champion for the top spot? It was Tarin electronics, and they're still there, vying for – and now winning – billion-pound contracts from the government."

"Won't the government stop them, now we can prove that they were behind the bomb?"

"I'm afraid not. All we can prove is that Helena Gunther was behind the bomb, and as I said before, no-one's going to reopen the case now that she's dead."

Parkes sat back and fell silent. I too could think of nothing positive to say and retired to my room.

***

The following morning I was woken just after six o'clock by Parkes knocking softly on my bedroom door.

"What is it?" I asked, "Have you heard from Sophy?"

"No, but you've got to come quickly. I've had a text from my dad."

I threw on some clothes and walked down the hall to Alvaston's bedroom, quickly but quietly enough to avoid waking my parents. Alvaston was already dressed and sitting on the bed with the chess set in front of him.

I took my usual position in the easy chair. "What did your dad say?"

"It won't make sense unless I first explain what he's doing in the Middle East. And once I've told you I can't un-tell you, if you see what I mean. We're heading into dangerous territory, Robert, and this might be your last chance to turn back."

"I'm in," I stated as calmly as I could. Parkes, who had been extremely tense, relaxed visibly, as if relieved that at least one person was with him on this particular journey.

"To cut a long story short," he began, "there's a strong and growing criminal organisation, headquartered somewhere here in London, that has been recruiting top scientists around the world. The organisation is covert, intelligence-led, tech savvy and utterly ruthless. Within a year Dad believes it will become the biggest threat our country faces. And within a decade the biggest threat to the whole world."

"What sort of threat?"

"That's just it – we don't know yet." I noticed the switch to first person plural. Clearly Alvaston was already familiar with – or already involved in – his father's investigation.

"Up until now," Parkes continued, "the group has concentrated on low-level financial scams, despicable schemes which prey especially on those elderly people who have yet to catch up with the age of computer banking. Each individual act might only net them ten or twenty thousand – small beer for them but enough to completely ruin the retirement plans of the victim. At first Dad thought it was just another criminal gang after a quick buck, but when he dug deeper he found that they have been doing this on a prolific scale, using the internet to replicate the same ploys in every country on every continent. And it has made them immensely rich – to the point where they now hold as much cash as a medium-sized bank."

"And what are they doing with all this money?"

"That's the strange thing. We think the financial scams are just the first part of a bigger plan, to provide the finance for something even more sinister, but the scientists they are recruiting are mostly experts in quantum mechanics – not the sort of field that lends itself to common or garden crime of any sort!"

I sat back and thought about this, but my own knowledge of quantum mechanics was limited to two poorly understood physics lessons halfway through last term – unlikely, I reasoned, to be sufficient to work out the intentions of a major international crime gang, so I changed the subject. "How do they recruit these people?"

They identify the people they want and send them a series of puzzles – the sort of puzzles only a quantum physicist could solve - and a meeting place and time. Solving the puzzles provides the password to use at the meeting, and that's where it gets interesting."

"Because?"

"Because for the last three months my Dad has been trying to get recruited! He's posing as a top British scientist called Professor Merton. The real Professor Merton is a long-time friend of my father's and is about to retire. Instead, he applied for a position at a top university in the Middle East, which provided an ideal opportunity for Dad to slip in in his place."

"And is it working?" It was one of many questions swirling around in my head.

"Yes I would say so – at least he's been teaching for three months now and the university still hasn't twigged that he doesn't actually know anything about the subject!"

"No – I mean have the criminal organisation tried to recruit him?"

"Ah – yes. Just yesterday, in fact, and that's why he texted us."

I refocused my thoughts. "But if this organisation is as ruthless as you say, trying to get recruited is a pretty dangerous game isn't it?"

"Life is dangerous, Robert, if you choose to live it!" But Alvaston didn't give me time to properly grapple with this philosophical statement before continuing with his story. "Dad was sent the puzzles and the meeting details yesterday, and the meeting is on Saturday, the day after tomorrow."

"So he only has two days to solve the puzzles and work out the password?"

"That's about the long and the short of it. He's made a good start though. He's already worked out that the password is an eleven-letter word, probably in English, and he knows that the first, third and last letters are M, S and Y respectively. That narrows it down to just 11 words, apparently. The problem is that most of the remaining puzzles require a depth of understanding of quantum mechanics that is quite beyond him, and asking another scientist like Professor Merton would be to put their life in danger too. That's why he needs our help."

"Our help?" suddenly this dangerous situation thousands of miles away in the Middle East was coming far too close to home.

"Yes. The only remaining puzzle that doesn't require specialist knowledge is the clue for the fifth letter, and it's a chess puzzle. Of course Dad could solve it given time but he also has to keep up his cover as a university lecturer and today and tomorrow the university is hosting open days in quantum mechanics, so he won't have any time to consider the puzzle."

"I'm texting it to you now so you have a record of the position," Alvaston continued, tapping the screen on his phone, "but I've also set it up here on the board. The text attached to the puzzle claims it came from a tournament in the run-up to Botvinnik-Bronstein in nineteen fifty-one but I don't believe it. The position is clearly contrived."

I looked at the board. As Parkes had pointed out, the position was obviously manufactured, with an almost symmetrical pawn structure on each side and many of the other pieces symmetrically placed. Also… "Just a minute, that can't be right. Both kings are in check at the same time!" I exclaimed.

Parkes, who had been allowing me time to take in the position, replied quietly "Yes, that's rather the point. The question is this: 'Two pieces have been knocked off the board by mistake. What are they and on which squares did they sit?'"

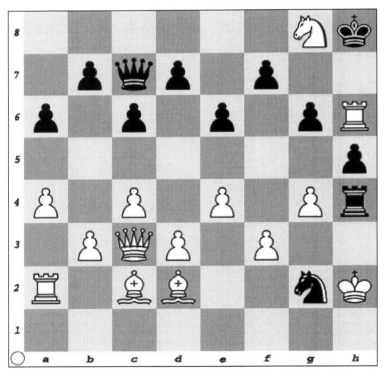

Figure 47. "Two pieces have been knocked off the board by mistake. What are they and on which squares did they sit?"

"Two pieces – surely that's impossible!" I exclaimed. "They could have come from anywhere!"

"Not from anywhere." said Parkes, getting up from the bed and walking over to the closet to put his shoes on. "You said yourself that both kings are in check, so that limits things a bit."

"It still looks pretty impossible to me."

"The heights yield to endeavour!" he replied. "There's very little that can't be solved with careful detective work, and I've been watching you, Robert – you've got a lot of experience now and you're well on the way to becoming a fully-fledged chess detective." He opened the door ready to step out into the hall.

I was immediately suspicious – Parkes had never before said anything to give the impression that I was anything other than a complete beginner at chess detection, and a rather slow one at that. "Wait - where are you going?" I asked.

"I have to go to Chigwell."

"That's near where Helen Gunther had the car accident, isn't it?"

"Exactly! After the accident they towed her car to a salvage yard in Chigwell. I want to find out whether the brake system had been tampered with prior to the accident."

"But your Dad – he might be in danger!"

"Sophy is also in danger. Two people are in danger, and there are two of us. We have to divide our labour. You must see that."

"But…"

"Look, you do have lots of experience now, and it's chess club today – you can talk it through with Mr. Wills, but only as a hypothetical problem of course! On no account are you to tell him anything about what's really going on."

"Yes I understand, but…"

"Look, I should be back sometime this evening. If the worst comes to the worst we can work on it together through the night, but for now I really need your help on this one. Can I count on you?"

I sat back and thought for a moment. I'd already given him my word, and now I had to make good. "Of course you can." I replied. "I'll do my best."

"Great!" said Parkes, smiling. Then he stepped out into the hall and closed the door quietly behind him.

Chapter 17. The Final Chapter

For the first hour at least I couldn't think about anything properly. Alvaston's story about his dad just kept going round and round my head. Much as I reminded myself that his dad had chosen this route without even consulting me, somehow I had become complicit in an activity that put his life in danger, and the weight of responsibility kept dragging my thoughts round in circles.

Black

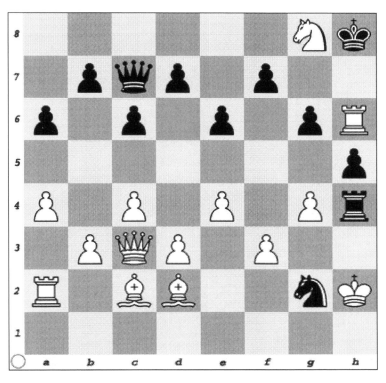

White

Figure 48. "Two pieces have been knocked off the board. What are they and on which squares did they sit?"

At eight o'clock Mum called me down to breakfast. Dad had already left for work, so it was just the two of us. Our conversation, as usual, crossed from school and how different it was now that all the lessons were on-line to friends and relatives, and then back to school again. The sheer normality of it gave me a break from the endless circles of 'what-ifs' and enabled me to gather my thoughts.

"Double chemistry at nine – don't forget!" she said at the end as I headed for the stairs.

"I won't!" I shouted back over my shoulder.

As soon as I got into my room I opened my laptop and logged into the lesson a quarter of an hour early to make sure I was marked down as present. I muted the mic and left the loudspeakers on at 50% - loud enough for a passing parent to think I was in my chemistry class, but quiet enough to block it out mentally in order to concentrate on the task at hand.

Coming back to the problem afresh I made some progress almost immediately. Both sides, I reasoned, were in check from two different directions at once. Therefore the two missing pieces had to block either both of the white checks or both of the black checks. I chose two of the pieces not currently on the board at random, the black rook and the white knight, and placed them on h3 and g3, blocking both checks on the white king.

It was immediately apparent, however, that the situation was still impossible. Black was still in check from two directions. Without the pawn on g6 that would have been possible: the rook could have moved from f6 to h6, but with the pawn on g6 there was no way white could deliver check from both directions simultaneously.

Black

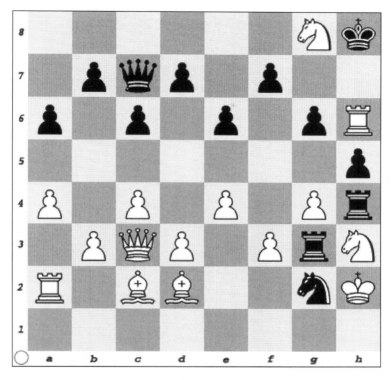

White

Figure 49. My first attempt. There was no way white could deliver check from both directions simultaneously.

I moved the pieces to g7 and h7. The situation was the same but with the colours reversed. There was now no way that black could deliver check from both directions at once.

Somehow, then, the two pieces must block three of the four checks, and then it hit me: *the only way that could happen is if one of the pieces were on e5, blocking the checks from both queens at once!*

I reset the position and placed the white knight from off the board on h3, but this time with the rook on e5. The position was beginning to look more sensible, with only one king in check, and from only one direction. But another problem immediately reared its head. Even without the extra check from the queen what move could white have made to deliver check with the rook?

Black

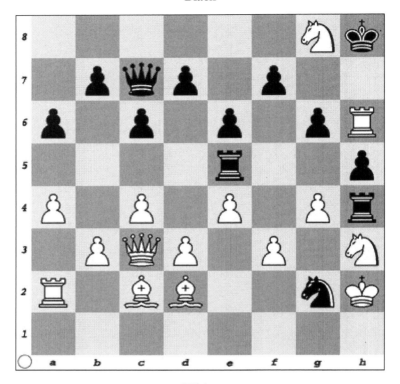

White

Figure 50. My second attempt. Even without the extra check from the queen what move could white have made to deliver check with the rook?

I swapped the knight from h3 to h7 and found the same question with respect to the white king. I tried every combination of the pieces off the board on the three squares e5, h3 and h7 but to no avail – I couldn't find a legal move leading to any of the positions.

Dr. Smith, my chemistry teacher, was still talking in the background and my mind drifted. I could see him on the laptop screen walking up and down in front of the blackboard and tried to imagine him talking to an empty classroom. I was even tempted to give up and finish the chemistry lesson. But life had changed recently. I left the laptop running and turned back to the problem, replacing the white knight on h3 and the black rook on e5 as before.

I stared at the position relentlessly, but it wasn't until the chemistry lesson had finished, and only half an hour before chess club opened, that I hit on the solution. The white rook couldn't have moved to deliver check, but a pawn on h7 could have taken a piece on g8 and under-promoted to a knight!

***

On-line chess club started at twelve o'clock sharp. Mr. Wills opened with an explanation about the on-line under-18 quickplay tournament that was to be held at the weekend and then busied himself pairing people for games. As ever there was a long queue of students wanting to play Mr. Wills himself and I had to wait almost half an hour before I could talk with him alone.

I explained that I had been given an interesting chess problem by Alvaston's dad. I didn't say anything about the background, and Mr. Wills didn't ask, but I could tell from his demeanour that he understood there was more to this than a simple chess puzzle.

The website we used for chess club had a facility for setting up chess problems, and I quickly entered the positions of the pieces. I gave Mr. Wills a few minutes to examine the position before briefly relating the progress I had made that morning. "Does that seem right to you?" I asked when I had finished.

"Yes I think so – at least I can't see any other solution. So you know the positions of the two pieces – that's a good start!"

"Yes, I know the positions, but I can't get anywhere in finding out which pieces they are. If we go back a move…" I swapped the knight on g8 for a pawn on h7, "…then all the pawns are on the board, so there can't have been any other promotions, which I think means that the two pieces must come from those that are currently off the board – either or both of the white knights, either or both of the black bishops, the black knight or the black rook."

"Yes I'm sure that's right," said Mr. Wills, "and the piece on e5 obviously can't be a black bishop, because the white king would still be in check - but that's the only thing I can see immediately."

After another five or ten minutes poring over the position other members of the club started signalling on the website that they wanted to talk with the teacher. "I've got to go," he said reluctantly, "but I think I might have spotted something useful - how did the pawn on h7 get to where it did? In particular how did it get past the black h pawn? Anyway, good luck with the problem. You're doing well and I'm sure you'll crack it!"

I left the website and turned to concentrate on this new line of attack. My thinking was interrupted, however, by Mum calling me down for lunch.

***

I started again just before two o'clock. How could the white h pawn have circumnavigated its black counterpart? After some thought I decided there were just three possibilities. Either the black h pawn took something on g6, allowed the white pawn to march past and then took something else on h5, or the white h pawn took something on the g file, passed the black h pawn and then took something else to move back onto the h file. The final possibility was that the white h and g pawns had swapped files – that the pawn on g4 might actually be the white h pawn – but I quickly concluded that there was no material difference between this and the second case – either way white needed at least two captures to get the pawn to h7.

I felt I was almost there, but I made no progress at all over the next three hours. Either black made two captures, which was quite possible because there were two white knights that could have been taken, or white made two captures, or three if you included the final capture on g8, but that was also quite possible because there were four black pieces no longer on the board. I found the same train of futile thoughts going endlessly round and round my head.

The answer, when it came, came in a flash of inspiration. I was looking idly at the pieces on the queen's side, away from the action on the h file, and noticed for the first time that black's b and d pawns stood on their original squares, which meant that black's white-squared bishop could never have moved: it must have been captured on it's own square. So if it were black's h pawn that went wandering, capturing the two white knights to swap to the g file and back, that left only black's rook, knight and black-squared bishop to be the two pieces knocked off the board from e5 and h3, plus the piece taken on g8. But Mr. Wills had previously pointed out that the black-squared bishop couldn't be the piece on e5 because the white king would still be in check. Neither could it be the piece on h3 or the one that stood on g8, because both of those were white squares.

I felt excitement rising, but forced myself to check my logic. If black's pawn had been the one changing files then the two white knights were accounted for, but I still needed three pieces, the two on e5 and h3 plus the one recently captured on g8. None of them could be black's white-squared bishop, because that piece never left its home square, and none of them could be black's black-squared bishop, leaving only two pieces for three positions. *So it couldn't have been black's h pawn that went wandering.*

The rest was trivial. If it wasn't the black pawn that went wandering, the white pawns must have made at least three captures between them including the one on g8. Given that black's white-squared bishop was captured on its home square, that accounted for the remaining black pieces, leaving just the two white knights. So that had to be the answer – the two missing pieces were white knights standing on e5 and h3 respectively!

I checked my logic for the whole problem three times before texting Alvaston. I knew better than to blurt out anything about criminal organisations in an open text and said simply "I've solved the puzzle."

Alvaston's reply was almost instantaneous. "Fantastic! I've also solved my puzzle. On the train back. Please tell your mum I'll be home for dinner."

Alvaston appeared at six thirty, just as I was setting the table. Much as we were eager to swap news we had no choice but to sit through the dinner-time conversation. Alvaston explained that he'd had to go back to his house to check on something or other, which was a lie but seemed to satisfy Mum and Dad. I had to explain what we'd done in chemistry that morning and found that, rather surprisingly, enough of Dr. Smith's monotonous droning had sunk in to allow me to put together a fairly convincing account. Mum had met a friend in town, but the coffee shops were all shut because of COVID-19. Dad had a bad day at the office. The usual conversation.

At the end of the meal I volunteered to clear the table and load the dishwasher. I had long known this to be the fastest way to escape after a meal, partly because the offer was always accepted and gave me a free pass from picking up other more time-consuming jobs, and partly because I could start swiping things off the table, bringing an immediate end to the meal itself.

"You first," I said when we got upstairs again. "What did you find about Helena Gunther's car?"

"It's bad news, I'm afraid. There was a big hole in the pipe carrying the brake fluid. It's not enough to take to the police, but one corner of the hole had serrations on, like it was nicked with a hacksaw. If you know where to do it you can make a small hole that doesn't stop the brakes from working, but when the fluid pressure gets high, which is when you're braking sharply at high speed, the whole pipe fails. And that, of course, high speed and braking sharply, is exactly when you need your brakes the most."

"So she was murdered!"

"Yes, she was murdered," repeated Alvaston quietly, "because someone knew we were getting close to the truth. But Sophy also knows the truth about the explosion, so she could be in real danger too."

We talked back and forth about Sophy's situation and what we could do to help, but neither of us could think of anything useful except to wait for her reply to Alvaston's message.

In the end Alvaston changed the subject. "What about you?" he asked. "How did you get on today?"

I set up the original position on the board and took Alvaston through my solution. He was nodding confidently all the while. When I got to the part about the pawn captures he raised one eyebrow, but still didn't say anything. When I finished my story he sat completely silent for about five minutes, his eyes scanning up and down the board searching keenly for any gaps in my logic.

"Absolutely brilliant! Well done, old chap!" he exclaimed finally. "I knew you could do it!"

I smiled, and watched as Alvaston texted his dad with the solution. After half an hour his dad responded with quite a long text, which Alvaston summarised for me. "He says thank you very much. Given that the two missing pieces were knights he's put an N as the fifth letter of the password. Apparently that reduces the number of possibilities from 11 down to just one!"

"And what's that?" I asked.

"Misanthropy. Hatred of mankind. What a very apt password for an international criminal organisation!"

We talked for an hour or so, discussing what the day's news meant for Sophy and for Alvaston's dad, but we were both tired after the day's work and I retired to my room.

***

The next morning Alvaston didn't come down to breakfast. That wasn't unusual. Under the lockdown rules we were allowed out one hour a day for exercise, and Alvaston always went for a run before breakfast. Just on occasion he'd do an extra circuit, which made him late. But when it got to ten o'clock and he still hadn't come home, I knew something was wrong.

I told Mum I was going out, grabbed my mac and headed up the hill to the cemetery. Alvaston had told me once that his run took him through the cemetery and he often stopped there if he needed to think something through. It was raining hard, and as I climbed the hill a violent wind blew up and the rain lashed in waves against my face.

I reached the entrance to the cemetery and turned into a long grassy drive leading to a small brick-built chapel. As I neared the chapel I saw Alvaston slumped on a bench just under a large stained-glass window. He wasn't wearing a coat, and as I came closer I could see that his clothes were completely wet through – God knows how long he had been sitting there in the rain.

"Alvaston, what's the matter?" I asked. Although I was standing right next to him I had to shout to make myself heard above the wind and the rain.

Alvaston looked up at me but said nothing. I noticed that he was clutching his mobile tightly in his left hand.

"Is it Sophy? Has she replied? Is she safe?" I shouted.

"Yes, she's replied!" he said, and lifted his phone to read the message again. Then he suddenly stood up next to me. "And I'm sure she's safe!" And as he said that he pulled the phone back and hurled it with all his might into the graveyard. It bounced once on the mud, hit a headstone and lay still.

"What did she say?" I ventured.

"Go and read it for yourself!" he replied. "In fact," he said, seeming to pull himself together, "be a good chap and take the phone back home. It has national secrets on, and I shouldn't leave it lying around."

I didn't want to leave him in that state, but I did go to retrieve the phone. The screen was cracked from bottom left to top right, but it was still working. I looked back at Alvaston before reading it. For some reason he was now standing upright on the bench, pointing straight at me and shouting. "She lied to me, Robert! She lied to me!" For a fraction of a second a lightning flash lit him and the chapel wall behind, followed quickly by a long low roll of thunder. Parkes collapsed once more into a heap on the bench, crying into his arms like a toddler.

I picked up the phone and just had time to read the message before the screensaver cut in. It was as concise as it was mean-spirited and heartless.

I LOVED MY AUNT.

NOW SHE'S DEAD AND IT'S ALL YOUR FAULT.

WHATEVER MOVE YOU MAKE, PARKES, YOU LOSE.

But as cruel as the message was, it wasn't those words that caused a tingling feeling to run up my spine. It wasn't those words that caused me to look plaintively towards Parkes, only to see that he was no use to man nor beast, and to decide I had to leave him there. It was the way Sophy signed off that made me realise that Alvaston was in mortal danger, that I too was in danger, that even my family was in danger, that I had to race home as fast as I could, that I had to get to my room as quickly as I could and to retrieve the scrap of paper I had hidden away just a few days ago, to contact the only person who just might be able to help.

It may not be a chess problem but I'm sure that you, reader, will understand the cause of my fear.

How did she sign off? With just her name.

SOPHY M. TARIN

Afterword and Acknowledgements

This book is partly inspired by a book I first came across in my late teens, "The Chess Mysteries of Sherlock Holmes" written by Raymond Smullyan. It quickly became a favourite and remains so to this day, almost forty years later.

I can see from browsing the internet that "retrograde analysis", the study of what's already happened to reach any particular chess position, has become something of an artform in itself. I can also see that there are a number of conventions that have grown up with it to provide clarity in certain situations that might otherwise be ambiguous. I have made no attempt to follow these conventions, but I believe I have provided enough information to avoid any ambiguity in the puzzles (or where there is intentional ambiguity I have made that clear in the text describing the problem).

I would like to thank Nigel Hosken for checking the logic of the puzzles. As a child I spent very many happy hours playing games with my father Donald Wilson and he taught me the rules of chess when I was quite young. It was Nigel, however, the Mr. Wills of my secondary school, who imparted a real passion for the game.

Even with the best proof-reading in the world errors can still creep through. Responsibility for any remaining errors, either in the puzzles or in the text, rests solely with me.

As a chess book, I hope it will appeal to chess players. To some it may appeal through the puzzles themselves, which is great. For me, though, the book is pure escapism – life would be so much simpler if every complex situation that life throws up could be reduced to the level of a single chess problem!

In any case, for whatever reason, I hope you enjoyed the book!

Alec Wilson, October 2020

Credits

The **chess diagrams** presented in this work were created using the website https://www.chessvideos.tv which refers to the BSD license which can be found at https://www.chessvideos.tv/diagram-license.

The **cover** was produced using the GNU Image Manipulation Program (https://www.gimp.org) which is freely distributed under the GNU General Public License.

The **newspaper clippings** were generated using a template from Presentation Magazine (https://www.presentationmagazine.com/editable-powerpoint-newspapers-407.htm).

The **author photo** on the back cover was taken by Charlie House (http://www.charliehousemedia.com).

Printed in Great Britain
by Amazon

53384865R00084